Now that the weather is warmer, you can relax in the sun with this month's collection of seductive reads from Harlequin Presents!

Favorite author Lucy Monroe brings you *Bought: The Greek's Bride,* the first installment in her MEDITERRANEAN BRIDES duet. Two billionaires are out to claim their brides—but have they met their match? Read Sandor's story now and Miguel's next month! Meanwhile, Miranda Lee's *The Ruthless Marriage Proposal* is the sensuous tale of a housekeeper who falls in love with her handsome billionaire boss.

If it's a sexy sheikh you're after, *The Sultan's Virgin Bride* by Sarah Morgan has a ruthless sultan determined to have the one woman he can't. In Kim Lawrence's *The Italian's Wedding Ultimatum* an Italian's seduction leads to passion and pregnancy! The international theme continues with *Kept by the Spanish Billionaire* by Cathy Williams, where playboy Rafael Vives is shocked when his mistress of the moment turns out to be much more.

In Robyn Donald's *The Blackmail Bargain* Curt blackmails Peta, unaware that she's a penniless virgin. And Lee Wilkinson's *Wife by Approval* is the story of a handsome wealthy heir who needs glamorous Valentina to secure his birthright.

Finally, there's Natalie Rivers with her debut novel, *The Kristallis Baby,* where an arrogant Greek tycoon claims his orphaned nephew—by taking virginal Carrie's innocence and wedding her. Happy reading!

Mediterranean Brides

by Lucy Monroe

*Two billionaires, one Greek, one Spanish—
will they tame their unwilling wives?*

Meet Sandor and Miguel, men who've taken
all the prizes when it comes to looks, power,
wealth and arrogance... Now they want
marriage with two beautiful women. But this
time, for the first time, both Mediterranean
billionaires have met their matches and
it will take more than money or cool to tame
their unwilling mistresses—try seduction,
passion and possession!

The MEDITERRANEAN BRIDES duet:

Bought: The Greek's Bride
Sandor's story
Available this month

Taken: The Spaniard's Virgin
Miguel's story
Out next month

Lucy Monroe

BOUGHT: THE GREEK'S BRIDE

Mediterranean Brides

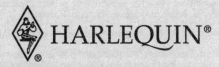

HARLEQUIN®

TORONTO • NEW YORK • LONDON
AMSTERDAM • PARIS • SYDNEY • HAMBURG
STOCKHOLM • ATHENS • TOKYO • MILAN • MADRID
PRAGUE • WARSAW • BUDAPEST • AUCKLAND

ISBN-13: 978-0-373-12636-1
ISBN-10:   0-373-12636-0

BOUGHT: THE GREEK'S BRIDE

First North American Publication 2007.

This edition published by arrangement with Harlequin Books S.A.

® and TM are trademarks of the publisher. Trademarks indicated with ® are registered in the United States Patent and Trademark Office, the Canadian Trade Marks Office and in other countries.

www.eHarlequin.com

Printed in U.S.A.

All about the author…
Lucy Monroe

LUCY MONROE sold her first book in September of 2002 to the Harlequin Presents line. That book represented a dream that had been burning in her heart for years—the dream to share her stories with readers who love romance as much as she does. Since then she has sold more than thirty books to three publishers and hit national bestseller lists in the U.S. and England. But since selling that first book, the reader letters she receives have touched her most deeply. Her most important goal with every book is to touch a reader's heart, and it is this connection that makes those nights spent writing into the wee hours worth it.

She started reading Harlequin Presents books very young and discovered a heroic type of man between the covers of those books—an honorable man, capable of faithfulness and sacrifice for the people he loves. Now married to what she terms her "alpha male at the end of a book," Lucy believes there is a lot more reality to the fantasy stories she writes than most people give credit for. She believes happy endings are really marvelous beginnings and that's why she writes them. She hopes her books help readers to believe a little, too…just like romance did for her so many years ago.

Lucy enjoys hearing from readers and responds to every e-mail. You can reach her by e-mailing lucymonroe@lucymonroe.com.

For my mom and sisters…because there is a love so strong and so unconditional it lights life even during the darkest moments and makes the joyful ones so bright, they are incandescent. That love is the one we share—a sister and mother's love is so precious and beautiful and I thank God that He put me in this family to share this deep love with you all. Always in Christ, Lucy—daughter and sister

CHAPTER ONE

HIS BIG, WARM HAND against the small of her back, Ellie allowed Sandor to guide her into the exclusive Boston restaurant. It felt good to walk into the air-conditioning. Boston in the summer was muggy and hot, but the instant cold sent shivers chasing along her arms and made her nipples bead behind the black silk bodice of her dress.

Rather than discomfort, her body reacted with a sensual pleasure that was her constant companion in this man's company.

It had marked their first meeting and had not abated since, leaving her with a need to explore a side to her character that she usually ignored. Her feminine sexuality. She found herself dressing more sexily around him than she ever had in the past and reveling in the small, possessive touches he peppered their dates with.

Tonight, she'd worn a dress by Armani that she loved because it was both elegant and sexy. Its sleeveless design and scooped neck left her arms, a good portion of her chest and her back exposed, but the hem swirled modestly below her knees. The black silk clung to her understated curves and the thin fabric offered no real barrier between his hand

and the sensitive skin of her back. And that single point of contact was enough to send her nerve endings rioting.

She had to concentrate on maintaining a bland façade for him and the other restaurant patrons, but she couldn't help wishing they were someplace private. Someplace she might actually get the nerve up to ask why he'd never pressed for deeper intimacy when his good-night kisses were powered by a wealth of barely leashed passion. Passion she'd decided she wanted to explore.

She recognized several faces as the maître d' led them to their table and wished she didn't. She would like to go out, just once, to a restaurant that was not one of the accepted watering holes for their kind. But Sandor Christofides demanded the best. In everything.

Sometimes, it made her wonder what he was doing with her.

She had been born to the world he had worked so hard to enter, but as far as she could see, that was all she had to offer him. At five foot nine, with small curves, average features, and rather boring dark blond hair, she was not particularly beautiful; she did little to cultivate the contacts others would kill to obtain; she abhorred the standards set by money and frequently refused to uphold them. Her job as an employment counselor for the state was as unglamorous as it got. Her clients wouldn't make it on to the "Who's Who" list of anything, for that matter…neither would she. Not anymore.

Her dad considered her career a complete waste of her Ivy League education, but she didn't care. She considered his overwhelming preoccupation with his business a waste, too. Not that she dismissed his company as unimportant, but she hated the fact that it always had and always would come before her, anyone or anything else.

Interrupting Ellie's thoughts, the maître d' stopped beside the same table they always had when Sandor brought her here. Its placement was an indication of Sandor's importance, something her father would take for granted, but she didn't think Sandor did. His dark brown eyes would glow with satisfaction for a brief moment at small things like this, as if they really mattered to him.

Which was another reason they weren't exactly well suited. Stuff like that just did not impress her. Maybe she was jaded by growing up around it, but she got a lot bigger thrill out of one of her clients getting a job, or a certification necessary to do so, or additional education.

She knew why she said yes to every one of Sandor's invitations. Because she was quite literally enthralled with the man. But she didn't understand why he kept extending them. Especially if he didn't want to sleep with her. He just didn't seem like the celibate type, but that might be her own libido talking.

Sandor seated her though typically the maître d' would have done so. She took it as a mark of his Greekness…or his possessiveness. She wasn't sure which, but for as little as she understood what Sandor saw in her, she knew she would not be the one to end their relationship. Because the little actions like him seating her personally made her feel special.

They also exhibited a side to his nature she found enticing. He didn't bow to the dictates of the world he inhabited, but insisted it take him on his terms. And when she was with him, she felt truly alive for the first time in her twenty-four years.

She couldn't help watching with a hungry intensity she tried to hide as he folded his six-foot-four frame into the chair across from hers. His dark, wavy hair, cut just a little long framed chiseled features she could stare at all night. His superbly muscled frame filled out his dinner jacket in a way few businessmen did.

His hands were well groomed, his nails buffed from a masculine manicure, but they were big and marked with tiny scars from a background very different to hers.

After placing their napkins in their laps, the maître d' left without giving them menus, but Sandor did not remark on it.

He was too busy looking at her, his knowing gaze acknowledging the desire she tried so hard to hide.

His even, white teeth slashed in a smile. "I am not on the menu, *pethi mou*." He paused and his smile turned to a predator's grin. "But I could be."

"Promises, promises…" she boldly teased back even as she felt the blush burning her cheeks.

Her body wasn't feeling any embarrassment, however. It was too busy reacting to his teasing as if to a caress. Unrepentant heat pooled low in her belly while her breasts tingled with the need to be touched. Her already hardened nipples felt like they increased in size, aching for his attention.

She wasn't precisely a virgin, but she'd never responded to anyone the way she responded to him.

He laughed, but didn't deny that he had no real plans to follow through on his taunt. The truth was, though they had been dating for three months, he had never pushed for the ultimate intimacy and he'd ignored her subtle hints in that direction.

She stifled a pang of disappointment and asked, "How did the negotiations go with the department store chain?"

He and her father had combined forces to try to lure one of the biggest worldwide retailers into using their combined shipping companies' resources and Sandor's import/export network.

"It is in the bag."

She loved the way he often talked American slang in his slight Greek accent. Unlike others of different nationalities that she'd met through her father, Sandor did not speak with the flawless accent of an Englishman, trained by exacting teachers. He'd told her he'd learned most of his English after coming to live in the United States when he was a child. His mother still spoke with a heavy accent that required a lot of concentration to understand sometimes. Luckily it was something Ellie was good at.

"I'm glad and I'm sure Dad is pleased."

"Yes, but we are not here tonight to discuss business."

"We aren't?"

"You know we are not."

She laughed softly. "I won't argue. I know more about my father's business since we started dating than I ever knew before and everything I do know, I've learned from you. I'm not exactly the best choice for a partner in that kind of discussion."

"But I think you are the ideal partner for other things."

Was he teasing her again…about the sex thing that she was fairly certain he had no plans to act on? Or did he mean something else? She looked at him in confusion, but though the corner of his mouth tilted enigmatically, he said nothing.

The waiter arrived at their table and poured them each a glass of Sandor's favorite wine. She liked it, too, and had never balked at his standing order for this particular predinner drink. But she was surprised when he confirmed their food order without asking her preference. He had never done that before. But then, both he and the waiter acted as if he'd ordered before even arriving at the restaurant.

That impression was further enforced when the waiter returned to their table seconds later with appetizers.

She sniffed appreciatively at the garlic baked shrimp dripping with melted butter and topped with a grated medley of three cheeses. "My favorite."

"I know." He put a piece of shrimp on a slice of baguette, carefully drizzling the garlicy butter over it and making sure there was just the right amount of melted cheese on top before handing it to her. "I know you very well, Eleanor."

"Do you?"

"After three months, do you doubt it?"

"That depends on what you mean. I think you do know a lot *about* me, but I am not sure you know *me*." Her dad would have known to order this appetizer, too, but that didn't mean he knew what made her tick. As far as she could tell, Ellie's dad had no desire to know her on any level but the surface.

She couldn't stifle the hope that Sandor would be different.

"Is there a distinction between the two?"

"Yes."

"If tonight goes as I plan, I will have a great deal of time to learn what *you* mean."

"And how do you plan for tonight to go?" Was he finally going to make love to her? Was she ready for it?

She almost laughed aloud at her inner voice. Ready? She was desperate for him. She'd already decided she wanted him, but the possibility of actually having him was throwing her into mental chaos. Which was silly. She wanted this man and while she had no intention of telling him that at this very moment, she would not lie to herself and pretend differently. She refused to indulge in those kinds of games.

"Allow me to reveal my plans in sequence."

She should have guessed he had an agenda of some sort. It was so like him. It was one of the more disconcerting ways he reminded her of her father. She didn't dislike it exactly, but it worried her a little. Were his agendas as coldly determined as her father's?

"By all means, I wouldn't think of attempting to divert your schedule."

He took a sip of wine, his dark eyes filled with mock menace. "Are you laughing at me?"

"Maybe, a little. Spontaneity is not your thing."

"You know me well."

"As well as can be expected after dating three months."

"Well enough." There was meaning behind his words, but she wasn't sure what it was.

"Aren't you going to have any of the shrimp?" she asked.

"I suppose, but the real pleasure comes from watching you eat them."

She had just taken a bite and her eyes closed in bliss. *Divine.* "To each their own."

He laughed. "I assure you, I am very happy with my own appetizer."

They were sharing the shrimp and he wasn't eating any, so it took her a second to understand his meaning. When she did, her eyes flew open. He was looking at her with a distinctly predatory light in eyes that had grown dangerously dark.

She took a deep breath, trying to calm the rapid pulse that was making her light-headed. Oh, my. When this man went for it, he held nothing back. She could not wait for later. Tonight, he would not leave her with a good-night kiss that made her toes curl and her body feel hollow with wanting. Not with that look in his eyes.

The appetizer was followed by butternut squash soup. She'd never had it at this particular restaurant before. "The chef must be trying something new."

"At my request."

"You *did* preorder the meal."

"Yes."

"Why?"

"Tonight is special, I want every aspect to be right."

"Special?"

"Yes."

"I like the sound of that." She smiled and took a bite of the soup he'd had one of the most temperamental chefs in Boston make just for her. "It's delicious."

"I would expect no less."

"I'm surprised you talked the chef into trying something new for your benefit alone."

"Money speaks most languages."

"Even that of a temperamental chef?"

"As you see." He indicated their twin bowls of the golden-orange soup. "But he did not make the soup for *my* benefit."

"No?"

"No. He made it for yours."

"At your request."

"Yes."

"Because tonight is special."

"Very."

She didn't know what else she would have said because at that moment, two things happened that derailed any thoughts of talking on her part. The first was that a trio of violinists took up residence in a spot near them that had on the last occasion they'd eaten there held a table of other diners. The musicians began to play a piece she had always found emotionally evocative and soothing at the same time.

The second occurrence was that she was presented with two dozen long-stemmed red roses by the maître d'. She took them and inhaled the scent of the perfect blooms. The heady fragrance bathed her senses.

She looked at Sandor. "They're beautiful."

"You are so certain they are from me?"

She laughed, her voice surprisingly husky. "Of course."

But she picked up the card to read anyway. It was small and white and read, "Sandor." Nothing else. He'd signed it himself, however. She recognized the black slashing writing.

"Thank you," she said, her face still buried in the roses. For some reason, she needed to hide there for a moment.

This was definitely more romance than she'd expected from him for the advent of the physical side of their relationship and it made her wonder if he had feelings for her she had not detected. The prospect sent a swarm of butterflies fluttering through her insides.

"It is my pleasure."

The maître d' took the flowers, returning moments later with them in a gorgeous crystal vase that he set at the side of their table.

She snuck peeks at them throughout the soup course, her mind spinning with what all this meant. Hope swirling through her along with a desire she gave herself permission to feel fully. Tonight, she would not go to sleep wishing for the moon, or Sandor's caresses. She was sure of it.

But when the main course was cleared—again a dish he

knew she enjoyed—a small black ring box appeared on the table and her breath ran out.

She stared at it. That couldn't be what she thought it was. The roses…the violinists… Suddenly her mind snapped with shattering clarity to a conclusion she had not even considered. The romance had been prelude to a proposal?

She couldn't believe it and yet, no other reason for the ring box could penetrate her racing mind. A man did not give a woman a ring simply to embark on an affair.

He reached across the table and took her hand. Feeling strangely numb, she could feel him looking at her and willing her to meet his gaze. She forced herself to do so, her eyes moving up the strong chin with its adorable cleft, past the long straight nose to a gaze as penetrating as a laser beam.

"Eleanor Wentworth, will you do me the great honor of becoming my wife?"

Even expecting the question, her usual aplomb deserted her and she gasped and stared, her mouth opening, but no sound emerging. He'd asked her to marry him, but she had no idea how he felt about her. If he loved her, wouldn't he have said it? Wouldn't she have sensed it?

He cocked his head to one side, one brow rising in an obvious prompt for a response.

"I don't know," she blurted out past a constriction of emotion in her throat.

The words sounded unnaturally loud to her ears. She couldn't believe she'd said it…like that. And from the look on his face, he couldn't, either. He had been expecting a very different response.

"Come, you must have been expecting this."

"Um…no, I wasn't. Honestly." She bit her lip, thinking

maybe she'd been naïve, but it had never occurred to her that a man as dynamic and sensual as he was would ask a woman to marry him that he had never slept with. "This has come as a complete surprise."

And she sounded more gauche than she ever had in her life. She'd been handling difficult social situations with grace since deportment classes when she was a mere six years old, but she'd never been proposed to…by a man she wanted, but was not at all sure wanted her. She hoped, had an inkling he might…but no certainty.

"An *unpleasant* surprise?" He didn't sound in the least vulnerable when asking that question. Not like she would have. Instead he sounded demanding, as if he wanted answers and he wanted them *now.*

"Not unpleasant." She shook her head, trying to clear it. "Just *very* unexpected."

"We have been dating for three months."

"Yes." They had already established that.

"Exclusively?"

"Yes…I mean I assumed…"

"For me, it has been exclusive."

Something inside her that she had not even realized had gone tense, relaxed a little. "For me, too."

"Where did you think this relationship of ours was going, if not marriage?"

"I thought maybe first…to bed," she answered honestly. Did they even have a relationship?

Casual dating yes…but a *relationship?*

He cursed in Greek. She recognized the word from a summer she had spent studying ancient civilizations in his former homeland. It was a very nasty curse. "I don't believe you just said that."

That caught her up short. "Why?" To her, it was a perfectly natural conclusion to make.

"It is unlike you."

"Perhaps you don't know me as well as you think you do." It might not be considered appropriate to discuss such matters in a public place, but she didn't give as much credence to proper behavior as everyone seemed to think she did. Or as her father thought she should.

Honesty was far more important to her.

And the fact was, he clearly did *not* know her all that well if he was shocked she'd had the temerity to mention sex. Marriage to a man who was that ignorant of her inner person was not a wholly appealing proposition. If it had not been *him* doing the proposing, it would hold no appeal at all.

"I do know you," he insisted.

Exasperated, she shook her head. "Not *that* way."

"I know enough to be certain of our compatibility."

"Because we've shared a few kisses?"

"We have shared more than kisses." His now molten gaze reminded her just how much more.

But as far as they'd gone, he always pulled back. Except once. The first time they'd kissed, it had almost gotten out of hand very quickly. Frightened by a wealth of emotion she wasn't used to experiencing, she'd pulled back. Since then, he had done more than kiss her, but he'd never let the passion flare so hot and he'd certainly never made love to her completely.

"Yes, we have, but it's the very fact that we've shared *just so much* that makes me wonder if we are as compatible in that way as you seem to think."

"Why should you wonder this? It is obvious that you want me." His Greek accent got thicker when he was upset.

She'd noticed that during a heated business phone call she'd overheard once, but it had never happened between them before.

She couldn't feel badly that it was happening now. She was glad to know she could make him angry. She needed the assurance that she could impact his emotions because he certainly impacted hers. Though she would much prefer evidence of another sort of emotion and she didn't appreciate his sentiment at all.

"Yes," she said between gritted teeth, "I do want you, but I'm not so sure you want me. And I'm not going to spend my life married to a man who is going to look for his passion outside of our marriage bed."

"Who said I would do this?" he demanded, his voice guttural and so thick with accent she had to concentrate to understand the words.

"Who said you wouldn't?"

"I say."

"I want to believe you, but—"

"There is no but. My honor is not in question here."

"I wasn't talking about your honor. I was talking about making love."

"You brought up the possibility I would violate the bonds of our marriage…that is a matter of personal honor and one I do not take lightly."

She was glad to hear that, but it didn't answer the real problem gnawing at her. He was business associates with her father, how much did that have to do with this marriage proposal? She simply couldn't convince herself that Sandor was suffering from shyness in admitting undying love. The man was far too confident…if he felt something for her, he would have said so. Yet, how did a woman ask if the man proposing was doing so as part of a business arrangement or if he wanted her personally? The blunt approach would probably be best.

Sandor wasn't the type to respond well to subtlety.

"Do you want me…I mean for my own sake, not simply because I'm my father's daughter?"

He frowned. "I would think that is obvious."

Maybe it was. To him. But it wasn't to her. When he kissed her, he made no effort to hide the barely leashed passion coursing through him, but he never acted on it. It confused the heck out of her.

"If it was obvious, I wouldn't be asking."

"I do want you." His voice dropped an octave, to a sexual purr. "Very much."

She licked her lips. "That's…that's good."

"But for me, the commitment comes first…then we make love."

She doubted he was a virgin, but apparently he ascribed to the standard some men still maintained about the women they intended to marry. "You've got some very old-fashioned views."

"Yes. I am not ashamed this is so. I was born in a traditional Greek village. My grandfather's beliefs may not find wholesale acceptance in me, but his influence is there."

"Sandor," she said, latching onto a topic less volatile to her emotions. "You never talk about your past. I don't know if your dad is dead, if your parents are divorced or why it is that you never mention your father, but your grandfather pops up in conversation on occasion. I know he's gone…at least I know that much," she muttered under her breath, "but I don't know why you and your mother live here in America. I don't know so much about you."

"Chief being the way I screw."

"*Sandor*," she hissed while her entire body blushed.

He glared. "I can be crude. Yes. It comes from the background you know so little about. But another thing comes from that past…the belief that a man does not take a virgin to his bed unless he is engaged to, but preferably married to her."

"Is that something your grandfather taught you?"

"He drilled it into me every day of my life while he lived. Only a man totally lacking in honor would do so."

"I see." She had a feeling there was a lot more to this topic she planned to explore, but first she was going to set the record straight on something else. "However, between us…the point is moot because I'm not a virgin."

"Of course you are."

CHAPTER TWO

"AND WHAT HAS made you draw this brilliant conclusion?" she demanded in a tone her dad would have recognized with trepidation.

Ellie didn't get mad easily, but once she was angry…she didn't back down.

"Look at the way you blush when we discuss sex."

"Married women blush. If that's your full supporting argument, you need to hone your deductive reasoning skills."

His eyes narrowed. "Do not play games with me about this. I know what I know."

"What you think you know."

"Stop this foolish claim. I am sorry if my observation has piqued your feminine pride, but I will never allow you to lie to me."

"Have issues with honesty do you?"

"Yes."

"That's surprising. Most businessmen at your level can be very inventive with the truth."

"But I will not tolerate untruth from those in my personal life. Ever."

"And will you give the same level of integrity to a relationship?"

"Count on it."

"In that case, let me repeat…I am not a virgin."

His jaw tautened and white lines appeared at the corners of his mouth. He was getting seriously upset by her adamant claim to sexual experience. "You have never had a serious relationship."

"Is that what my father told you?"

He didn't even look uncomfortable at being accused of talking about her in very private terms with her father. "Yes."

"Well, he obviously doesn't know everything about me, which should hardly come as a surprise." He had to have seen ample evidence during the time they'd been dating how far from close she was with George Wentworth.

"He has reason to know certain things."

"You mean the bodyguards I supposedly no longer have?"

Sandor managed to look slightly chagrined. "You know about the security service?"

"Of course." She rolled her eyes. "Please. Just because I told my dad I didn't want a bodyguard any longer doesn't mean he listened to me, but at least with them as silent and *distant* watchers, I have a little more privacy than I did when my bodyguards remained within touching distance."

"Not *that* much privacy."

He meant not enough for her father not to know if she had a man stay the night or had done so with one. "I don't have to sleep over with a man to have sex with one."

"But you would have to have had a relationship that went beyond a few casual dates because you are not the type of woman to sleep with a man on a whim."

"You're so sure about that?"

"Yes."

She couldn't deny it because he was right. And she did

not lie. Like him, she hated lies. Like the lie when a person told you they loved you but didn't. Not really.

"So…I have had more than one relationship that lasted a few months. I'm twenty-four years old, after all."

"But none of those relationships were deep."

"How do you know? My father said so," she guessed. "You can't trust the judgment of a man who thinks that balance sheets are more comprehensible than people. He doesn't *know* me."

"Like I do not know you?"

"I'm afraid so, yes."

Sandor shook his head with an impatient jerk. "You are wrong."

But she wasn't. Sandor did not know her any better than her father did, which meant he couldn't care for her any more deeply than her dad. While the knowledge hurt, it also really begged the question why Sandor wanted to marry her.

He was looking at her as if he expected another argument, but she didn't have to convince Sandor of her point of view. In this instance, it was her opinion that mattered and his confident insistence wasn't going to change it.

"I am not relying on his word alone," Sandor said. "I had you investigated." His expression showed not even a hint of remorse at the claim.

"What? *Why?*"

"When I first started considering you as a potential wife, I thought it prudent."

"You are kidding."

"No."

"I would have thought you too arrogant to believe you needed anything besides your own reading of a person in a situation like this."

"You have called me arrogant before."

"Have I?"

"Yes, the time I told you who would win the Super Bowl."

"You were so sure you were right and you aren't even a football fan."

He shrugged. "And yet I *was* right."

"Well, you're wrong about me being a virgin." And as much as the memories of the reason for her lack of innocence hurt, she felt a certain grim satisfaction in catching him in the wrong.

Maybe she should be offended he'd had her investigated, but she wasn't. She was, however, bothered. If Sandor wanted a relationship with her, why hadn't he made the effort to get to know her better rather than having her investigated? Maybe it wouldn't be so worrisome if he'd done it in addition to the investigation, but he hadn't.

The similarities to her dad were piling up and not in a good way. She'd been raised by a man who would have done the exact same thing in such a situation, who even now kept her under constant surveillance—ostensibly for her safety's sake. After all, she was the daughter of a very wealthy and influential man. However, he wasn't above using that so-called security to monitor more than her safety. She didn't know what her father thought his knowledge was going to do for him.

If he wanted a better relationship with her, he wasn't going to have it via a silent security detail. Only maybe that was just the way he liked it. He felt like he was doing his fatherly duty without getting emotionally involved.

"My investigator is very thorough," Sandor said, breaking into her derailed thoughts.

"Even the best investigators make mistakes."

"Perhaps." But she could tell he didn't believe her.

Instead of annoying her, it made her laugh. "We could go back to my apartment and I could prove it to you."

He looked far from amused. His dark eyes glinted with a warning she had no intention of heeding. "Are you trying to shock me, *pethi mou*?"

"Challenging you, I think." Recklessness filled her to bursting.

She didn't know if it came from the unexpected proposal that had mentioned not one word of love, from memories she'd prefer to forget, or from the renewed evidence that her father wanted no emotional connection to her, but the strictures of a lifetime were falling like dominos around her.

No, she wasn't the type of woman to view sex casually, but she wasn't a virgin and she was darned if she would marry a man who could turn himself off from her so easily. She didn't want Sandor to be like her father. She couldn't stand for their relationship to be as cold and distant.

"Why do you feel the need to challenge me?" he asked, sounding baffled.

It was almost cute, in an arrogant, macho reaction to what should have been a straightforward topic kind of way.

"Why don't you want me enough to have seduced me?" Or even accepted her sometimes not too subtle invitations?

"I told you."

"You believe I'm a virgin, so that puts me off-limits until the wedding night."

"Essentially…yes. Perhaps not until the wedding night, but definitely until the wedding is a date on the calendar."

"This is not the Dark Ages."

"Integrity has no time limit."

"Is that one of your grandfather's sayings?"

For a second his eyes burned with a pain that could not be mistaken. "As a matter of fact, yes."

"I don't understand why you want to marry me. You don't love me."

"And your friends have all married for the sake of some ephemeral emotion that cannot even be counted on to last past the cooling of the sheets in most cases?"

"No." She wouldn't pretend that all her acquaintances had married because they were in love. "But they aren't me and I happen to believe in that *ephemeral emotion*. I want more from marriage than a businesslike merging of two people's lives." She wanted more from life than that, period…but had no idea how to get it.

Other people found love so easily, but not her. But that didn't mean she had given up hoping to find it.

"And you will have more. We are compatible, in every way. We will have a family. You even enjoy my mother's company."

"She's easy to like, but you say that like it's a major consideration."

"Since I choose to have my mother live near me like a good Greek son, it is."

"I wouldn't mind living with your mother, but I'm not so sure about her son."

"So, you *are* considering my proposal?"

Was she? Her heart beat too fast, the pain of uncertainty squeezing her chest tight. She *was*. No matter what he believed about love, she was afraid she was already irrevocably in love with him—or headed there fast. What a hopelessly terrifying thought. "Yes, but I can't give you an answer right now."

"Surely you were expecting this."

"Funnily enough…I wasn't. I told you that."

He sighed. "Yes, but I would have thought you would have at least considered the possibility."

She just shrugged, not knowing what to say. They'd already been over the whole sex thing and their views were polar opposites. She'd been sure he wasn't ready for a deeper relationship because he hadn't pursued that angle and he'd assumed she'd realize he wouldn't pursue it until she was committed to him.

"And you cannot make the decision now, knowing what you know of me, of yourself?"

"No." Because if she did, it would have to be *no*. And her heart both demanded and rejected that answer.

"Is it my background?"

She stared at him. "I don't know enough of your background for it even to be a consideration and I hope you aren't implying I'm some sort of snob who would only marry someone born to the same world of privilege I was."

"I am not saying that, no. In fact, your refreshing refusal to judge others based on where they come from appeals to me greatly."

"I'm glad, because I don't want to change that part of me."

"But you are willing to change in other ways?"

"People grow…change is inevitable, but that's with me to stay."

"I am glad."

"But you are annoyed I won't accept your proposal right now."

"Not annoyed…disappointed. I would think you could see the advantages to a marriage between us."

He was disappointed, but not hurt. Which meant his emotions were not involved at all. That did not bode well.

She bit her lip, realizing she must have done so before because it felt tender. It was a bad habit, but she had enough to think about without trying to break it at the moment.

"I'm sorry. I'm not like you and my father. I don't make personal decisions based on business logic."

"What do you base them on?"

"Emotion."

His lips twisted with distaste just as she knew they would. He and her father had a lot in common. Maybe too much. She suspected he would be no more impressed with an emotional commitment from her than her father was.

She took a fortifying sip of water. "I know. That's a dirty word to you and men like my father, but it's how I live my life. You'll have to give me some time to think."

Silence pulsed between them until he pushed the ring box across the table. "Put it in your bag. We'll discuss the proposal again later."

She wasn't sure why he wanted her to take possession of the ring. Maybe he thought that since possession was nine-tenth's of the law, if she took the ring, she might have a harder time saying no and giving it back. The man was wily enough to have considered every angle.

"Please keep it until I give you my answer."

"I'd rather you kept it."

"Even if I say no?"

"I had the ring made for you. Whatever your answer, it is meant to be yours."

Unable to hold back from looking after such a statement, she opened the box. It was a square-cut precious stone exactly the color of her eyes. Aquamarine-blue. To either side was a perfectly cut square diamond of crystal clarity, only slightly smaller than the center stone.

Emotion that had no place in their discussion welled inside her and she husked, "It's beautiful."

"Like you."

She shook her head, dislodging the empty words. "I'm hardly that."

"After all we have said about honesty tonight, you think I lie about this?"

"I think you want to flatter me, but I have a mirror. I'm passable, but I am not beautiful. You should see pictures of my mother. She was beautiful." And she'd taken what existed of George Wentworth's heart to the grave with her.

"You know the saying, beauty is in the eye of the beholder."

She barely kept from rolling her eyes. "Yes."

"You are beautiful to me, Eleanor."

"False flattery isn't going to get me to agree to marry you."

"It is not false." His voice was a low rumbling growl. She'd managed to make him mad again.

"If you say so."

"I say so. Your beauty is timeless and very alluring to a man with my background."

"I don't understand." What did his background have to do with it?

"You are kind. Truly compassionate. You seek to make life better for those born without your advantages. Your care for others is ingrained to the depths of your soul. In that, you remind me much of my mother. Physically you are perfect to me. Your features are soft and feminine, your body a delight to my senses, but particularly that of sight. Yet, as much as you spark my desire, you are elegant and refined, even in jeans and a T-shirt. These things are beautiful to me."

She didn't know what to say. She could tell he meant

the words and that did something to her insides, tipping over a heart that had teetered on the precipice of love straight into its warm, sweet depths. Because as much as she'd learned he did not know about her, he had just proven he did know something about the woman she was under the skin and behind the image of a wealthy man's daughter.

"Private schooling and deportment training can do wonders," she said, trying to laugh it off while her heart contracted and expanded with her newly acknowledged feelings until she was dizzy with it.

"You were born with these traits, they are not something a person can learn."

She didn't agree. "You learned."

"I am far from compassionate and kind."

She'd seen the way he treated his mother. "I don't agree, but that's not what I'm talking about."

"What then?"

"How to fit the society we move in." She indicated the rest of the restaurant with a wave of her hand.

"But I do not fit."

"You do."

And yet, in a way he was right. He wore his suit, which was by a top designer and handmade, like he'd been born to it, but there was an aura of power around him that came from hard work and determination, not being born to wealth. His slight Greek accent. His direct way of speaking. They all spoke of a man not born to their world, but made.

But then she didn't fit her world perfectly, either. All her little idiosyncrasies stemmed from the inside and only showed themselves on close inspection. In that they were alike.

"Tell me about your childhood."

His eyes widened. "Why?"

"I want to know."

His jaw hardened. "And if I do not want to tell you?"

"I'll have you investigated." She grinned at his shocked expression.

And then he laughed and she fell just a little harder as she laughed with him.

"I was born in Greece."

"I knew that," she teased.

"We lived there, with my grandfather, until I was ten."

"We?"

"My mother, she was his only child, and I."

"Where was your father?"

"Gone."

A day ago, she would have respected the boundaries she sensed he'd erected, but a day ago, he had not asked her to marry him. "What do you mean, gone?"

"He was an American tourist. On the island for only a couple of days. By the time my mother realized she was pregnant, he was long gone. She did not even know his last name." Sandor did not sound condemning...of his mother at least.

"That must have been very difficult for her."

"Yes. But it could have been worse. My grandfather did not kick her out of the family home despite the shame her condition brought him. He supported her and me in the years that followed."

At what cost though? Definitely Sandor had not come out of that home unscathed.

"What about your grandmother?"

"She had died the year before. Grandfather often said that it was a lucky thing, for the shame would have killed her."

"He sounds like he was a harsh man."

"He was. In some ways. But he loved my mother and he took care of her even though what had happened went against his entire belief system."

"She was young." Hera Christofides had to have been a teenager when she had Sandor because she barely looked forty now. She had to be older than that, but Ellie was guessing it wasn't by much.

"She was sixteen. Grandfather forgave her, but he never forgave the man who made her pregnant."

"The *only a man without honor would take the virginity of a woman he's not married to,* thing?"

"Yes. And that man's blood runs in my veins."

She wondered if that was something else his grandfather had maintained, but she didn't ask. She merely said, "You can't know he wouldn't have stood by her, if he'd known about you, I mean."

"He knew she was a virgin, but he left her. He never returned to check on her. He did not care."

"Maybe. He probably wasn't much older than she was. There might have been reasons for why he didn't come back."

"Yes. Those reasons were that he *was* an irresponsible teenager himself who should have kept his pants zipped if he wasn't prepared to deal with the aftermath."

"Like you said, he was a teenager. It probably never occurred to him that there even was an aftermath."

"Ignorance does not change the outcome."

"No, it doesn't, but I have a hard time believing that any man who fathered you could have been totally without a sense of responsibility."

"I get my sense in that direction from my grandfather and mother."

"You can't know you got nothing from your father… since you didn't know him." She didn't know why she argued, only that is seemed important to make him realize life was not as black and white as his grandfather had obviously taught him it was.

"What is this about? Are you worried bad blood will tell?"

She sighed. "I hate that saying. It's just so wrong. Even if he was an all out jerk without a bit of good in him, that has no bearing on who you are today."

"Not everyone sees things that way."

"I know, but I'm the one who is right."

"And perhaps I am not the only arrogant one at this dinner table."

"Knowing when I am right is not arrogance," she teased.

"I will have to remember that defense."

"You do that, but somehow I don't think it's a new concept for you."

He just smiled.

"For the record, I for one am glad your dad didn't keep his pants zipped and I bet your mom doesn't regret it, either."

The smile disappeared and his expression looked hewn from granite. "Why would you say such a thing?"

"Because, if he had, *you* wouldn't be here."

"And you think that is a good thing?"

"Yes, and I'm sure your mom agrees."

"But you hesitate to marry me."

The man was tenacious. "My reasons have nothing to do with you not being a pretty amazing person I'm glad is alive."

He raised his brows at that. "Then what are your reasons?"

"More to the point, what are yours?"

CHAPTER THREE

"I HAVE EXPLAINED...I find you beautiful inside and out. I am ready to marry and have a family. I want to do that with you." Sandor knew instinctively that if he mentioned the business deal with her father, it would make Eleanor balk.

It was not the overriding reason for him choosing her to be his wife, but it had played a role. That did not bother him, but he suspected she would react very differently to that knowledge. As she had said, she did not make her decisions based on the same considerations that swayed men like him and her father.

She wanted an emotional reason for marrying him. She wanted to be loved. He had gleaned that much, but that was not something he could give her. It was not something he wanted to give her. Love was an overrated emotion he preferred to steer clear of. He had loved his grandfather and he loved his mother, and that love had come with a price. He had paid in vulnerability when nothing else and no one else got to him.

His mother's unhappiness hurt when he let nothing else touch him. His grandfather's disapproval left wounds he swore no one else would ever get the chance to emulate. He would have to convince Eleanor there was enough going for them without the love he wanted no part of.

"My mother said she fell in love with my father at first sight." He didn't know why he'd mentioned that, but it supported the argument he was about to make, so he did not regret it. "The emotion you think such a panacea for pain is in fact one of the biggest instigators of it that I know. Her love led her into his bed. My grandfather's love kept her with him even though he could never overlook her indiscretion completely. His love for me drove him to push me harder, to demand more of me than he would have his own son. He would not allow me to become like the man who had sired me. Irresponsible and without honor. But his lessons were often painful and I knew they were born of love."

"Love does not always lead to pain."

"Yes, it does, and I do not want the pain that is inevitably born of love in my marriage."

She gasped and he grimaced. He had said more than he intended, but if it helped to convince her, he would not begrudge her the truth.

"What *do* you want?" Her sea-blue eyes were filled with a softness that called to something deep in his soul.

It had from the first moment he'd seen her across a crowded charity ball. She'd been with her father and Sandor had been instantly intrigued by this woman who was so clearly of the world he wanted to conquer, but not like it.

"I want children, a legacy—a legitimate legacy, to inherit what I have built, to build onto it. I want to please the woman who sacrificed so much to give me life and keep me with her. Even in Greece thirty years ago, a woman could find ways to end an unwanted pregnancy, but she never even considered it."

"How do you know?"

"I asked."

The compassion he liked so much sparked in Eleanor's eyes. She was exactly the kind of woman he wanted to spend the rest of his life with. A woman who could help to calm the demons that raged in his soul.

"Your mom wants you to marry?"

"You know she does."

Eleanor smiled. "Well, she's not very subtle…but I figured she hinted that way to all your dates."

"Actually, no."

"You mean I'm special?" she asked facetiously.

"Yes. She has hinted at me enough, but never to one of the women I dated. Until you."

"She wants grandchildren. A lot."

"Yes. What about you?"

"I'm too young to be a grandmother."

That was one of the things he really enjoyed about his little Eleanor. She teased him. She made him smile and she was always ready to do so herself.

"I meant do you want children?" He did not doubt her answer, she was too perfectly suited to motherhood not to want to be one, but he wanted to hear her say it.

"Yes. Very much."

"I thought as much."

It was her turn to grimace. "You think you know everything."

"Apparently I do not. I thought you would accept my proposal without a lot of fuss."

"Fuss?" she asked delicately and suddenly he knew he was treading on very shaky ground.

"I did not think it would be a difficult decision for you to make," he amended.

"It would have been easier if you had said you loved me."

He could only respect her courage and her honesty. "Do you want me to say it?"

"A lie of expediency designed to get you the outcome you want? What of your insistence on truth from me? I told you I won't accept any less."

Yet, he had a sneaking suspicion that they defined honesty differently. He dismissed the niggling worry and said, "I will give all the loyalty and dedication to your happiness a man who professes such feelings would do. There would be no lie in my saying the words if you need them to feel more comfortable about our marriage."

"Except that you don't feel the emotion and neither do you want to feel it. They'd still be a lie, Sandor."

"But the intent behind them, my dedication to your well-being, is not a lie."

"I understand that we see things very differently. Not only do you not want love, but I'm not sure you believe in romantic love at all or you could not blithely talk about saying the words as if that's all they were. Mere words."

"Romantic love is not something I have any personal experience with."

Pain flashed in her pretty blue eyes, but was gone so quickly, he could not be sure he had seen it.

"Will it help if I promise I will never say those words to another woman?"

"Can you promise that? What if you fall in love? Just

because you don't love me doesn't mean you are in-capable of loving someone else."

"I do not want to love anyone else."

"It doesn't always come with a choice."

He did not agree. "I keep my promises. It is up to you to decide if you trust me to do so."

"I do trust you."

A flare of triumph coursed through him.

She saw it and frowned. "I'm not saying I'm going to agree to marriage, but I think I'm beginning to understand why you asked me at least."

"I would have thought that was obvious."

"There you go being wrong again. This can't be good for your ego, but your reasons for picking me to share the rest of your life with are far from obvious."

"You will tease me one time too many," he warned on a mock growl.

"And you'll do what?"

"Perhaps I will make love to you and slay that dragon of doubt at least."

"Do you think a planned seduction will decimate my concerns about the fact that you find it so easy to control your libido around me?"

"I think, little one, that there are depths to you that I have yet to plumb." It startled him to have her take him to task for such a thing, but it also aroused him. "Trust me, I do not find it easy to control my desire around you, merely necessary."

"Because you don't want to be like your father."

"That is one reason."

"Tell me another."

"If you do not want to marry me, I do not want to spend my life addicted to a body I have no access to."

She burst out laughing as he'd meant her to, but there was a grain of truth to what he said. If he made love to her, he did not think he would ever want to let her go.

On the other hand, making love might be the very solution to their impasse. He would prove his passion to her and regardless of what she wanted him to believe, he knew she would only accept him into her body if she was making a major commitment to him.

He had already made his commitment to her and while he'd rather they were officially engaged with a wedding date set before he took her to bed, he had no doubts about the ultimate outcome. He was not taking advantage of her. They would marry. He was not a man who allowed anyone or anything to thwart him when it came to getting something he wanted.

And he wanted Eleanor Wentworth as his wife.

When they arrived at Ellie's apartment, Sandor requested her key card to park in the visitor's area of the secure garage under her building.

"Are you planning to come up for a while?" she asked as he pulled into a parking slot.

He waited until she looked at him to ask, "Are you planning to invite me?"

She usually did, but tonight she'd hoped to have some time to think.

He reached out and cupped her nape. "Invite me up, *pethi mou*. I am not ready for the evening to be over."

Just as it did every other time, his slightest touch impacted her senses with the power of a Level 10 earthquake.

"Even though it didn't have the outcome you wanted?"

she asked breathlessly, knowing she would not turn him away if he was intent on staying.

"You did not refuse me. It is enough."

"Is it?"

"I learned early to be patient when going after something I wanted. Rushing the outcome can sour it faster than facing opposition."

Why did the unabashed business-speak liquify her insides? She shouldn't be reacting to corporatese as if he'd said something intoxicatingly alluring, but the problem was that he'd said it in that low, sexy voice that had been shaking up her equilibrium since the first time she heard it. And, in effect, his sentiment *was* sensual. He was talking about convincing her to marry him, which *would* land her in his bed. Even if unbridled passion had not.

"I see. So, I'm a corporate merger you'd like to make?" she asked, trying to keep it light…trying to temper her own reaction to what shouldn't be nearly so much temptation.

"You are the woman I would like to marry, not a company I plan to buy—but the similarities exist, yes."

She couldn't help smiling wryly. Of course he would see most of his life in business terms. It was all he knew, that and the lessons on integrity he'd learned at his grandfather's knee. She shivered when she thought what it must have been like to be raised by a man who loved him, but not enough to see past his illegitimate birth. A man intent on making sure that what he considered *bad blood* would not show itself in his grandson.

If the older Christofides were alive today, Ellie would have a few choice words for him. But then if he were alive, Hera probably would never have left Greece and taken her son with her. Ellie and Sandor would never have met.

Coming on the heels of her inner revelation regarding her feelings for him, the thought chilled her.

"Come up," she said on a defeated sigh.

Sandor had not conquered her desire to be alone and think; her own conflicting needs undermined it. She wanted to spend time with him. She craved his presence like a drug and was just glad he wasn't one. She'd always thought she had a strong sense of self-control, but when it came to Sandor, she lost touch with it and her sense of self-preservation as well.

Which was one very good reason for not giving him an answer to his proposal tonight.

He climbed out of the car and came around to open her door. Always the gentleman, even more so than a lot of men born to money, social elevation and manners. He helped her from the car, transferring his hand to the small of her back once she was standing. She realized he did that a lot, this guiding her where he wanted her to go with a possessive-protective hold.

He kept his hand on her even in the elevator. He did that a lot, too…simply touching her for the sake of doing so, not because he needed to. He touched her like she was already his. It was one of the reasons she had been so confused over him not pressing to make love.

She understood better now, but wasn't sure that with understanding came acceptance.

Silence reigned in the elevator on the way to her fifth-floor apartment and no one else joined them to break it. It wasn't an awkward silence, but she was lost in her own thoughts and she sensed that Sandor was content to leave her that way.

He waited patiently for her to open her apartment door

and deactivate her alarm with the code and her thumbprint. The double locks on the solid steel door molded to look like a classic paneled wood door undid with a *snick*. She pushed the door open and led him inside.

"I like the security here."

She laughed. Sometimes, she got the impression that, like her father, Sandor considered the security at the Denver Mint no more than routine. "I picked out the apartment in a secure building to help Dad make the transition to me no longer living at home. That wasn't good enough for him. He gave me a security system installed by Vitale Security for a housewarming gift."

"I have used that firm before myself. They are very good."

"I'll say and the installation expert was to-die-for gorgeous."

"Was he?" Sandor asked in a rough voice.

"Totally delicious." She licked her lips. "But too short for me. He came all the way from the head office in Sicily. Dad demanded the best."

"I must then be grateful I inherited some tall genes somewhere, hmmm?"

She eyed his six-foot-four frame. "I bet that's one good thing you got from your father."

Sandor frowned, but he didn't deny it. Considering the fact that his mother was barely over five feet, maybe he couldn't.

"We all inherit things from our parents, and we hope they are the best things," she said as she led him into the living room. "I got my dad's stubbornness. Just ask him."

Sandor waited until she sat down on the bright yellow leather retro sofa before settling right beside her. "I have no need, having seen ample evidence of it myself."

She laughed again, loving just being there with Sandor at

that moment in time. She kicked off her sandals and curled her feet under her, turning her body slightly so she faced him.

He wasn't smiling in response to her laughter. Instead he was looking at her like he was trying to piece together what made her tick. "You're very understanding of George's need to protect you."

"I love him." She sighed. "And I understand that as the sole heir to a man as wealthy as he is that I'm a good candidate for a kidnapping."

"Yet you insist on living alone."

She barely stifled the urge to snort. "I don't exactly live alone, do I? His security team has the next apartment over. They monitor me as well as my apartment while I am gone."

"Wouldn't it be easier to simply live in your father's home?"

"Maybe, but while it may not be perfect, I have a lot more independence than I would have if I had stayed at home." It was also easier to convince herself that the reason she saw so little of her father was that they lived apart, not because he didn't care enough to make any time for her. "Besides, I really don't want my dad's money dictating every aspect of my lifestyle."

"You would prefer to be able to live without the security detail."

"Yes."

"But you make the concession to George's *feelings*—to his fears for you."

"And to practicality. But don't you do the same, for your mother?"

He smiled, laying one arm along the back of the couch. "Touché."

His scent enveloped her, the subtle fragrance of his spicy

aftershave mixed with his own essence. She'd read that a woman's sense of smell was more refined than a man's but it was the first time *she'd* ever noticed the individual scent of another person. Maybe it was because to her senses, Sandor was infinitely unique. In every way.

His warmth and sexy masculinity called to her and she forced herself to speak instead of closing the distance between their bodies. "I bet you find it as difficult to carve time out of your work schedule to have the family dinners and the excursions Hera insists on as I do to allow my dad to keep a security detail watching over me."

"I think you are right, though I never considered it in that light. I only know that since I was a small boy I was determined to give my mother the life my father *should* have." Something in his expression said his words surprised him as much as her.

He was an intensely private person, that he had shared as much of himself as he had with her was incredibly special.

Allowing herself one tiny touch, she brushed his arm and smiled. "Well, I'd say you surpassed that goal and then some."

"You think?"

She smiled with emotion shining in her eyes because it sounded like he really was asking the question. As if there could be any doubt. "I doubt your dad is a hugely wealthy tycoon and I'm certain he wasn't as a teenager. You've surpassed anything he could have done for her, even if he had stuck around."

"I think you may be right." The wealth of satisfaction in his voice told Ellie something else about this enigmatic man who wanted to marry her.

He had things to prove to himself…to his grandfather…*and* to the father he'd never met.

Remembering her role as hostess, she asked, "Would you like coffee…or an after dinner drink?"

"Neither, thank you."

Now, why did the way he said that make shivers dance along her nerve endings? "It was your idea to come up," she reminded him.

"To settle one of your concerns in regard to marriage, not because I crave more liquid refreshment."

"You plan to settle my fears?" How very noble of him. "In what way?" Though she thought she could guess.

He leaned forward, invading her personal space completely and his body heat called to her while his dark eyes mesmerized. "Guess."

"What about the no sex before marriage integrity thing?" She'd meant to ask the question in a sarcastic tone, but her voice came out breathless and much too inviting. Darn it.

"I plan to marry you. It is up to you to set the date." He might as well have shrugged, he sounded so casual in that pronouncement.

And right then she realized he really did plan to marry her. Not hope. Not want. But the man had a *plan* and was fully confident in his eventual success.

"So, it's okay to seduce a virgin if you intend to marry her?" Again that breathless voice that was really starting to get on her nerves.

She sounded like she wanted his reassurance, but she didn't. Did she? Not this way…not planned. But Sandor was a planner and he worked best with a schedule. She'd known that since the beginning. She just hadn't expected it to dictate this part of their relationship.

"You have said you are not a virgin." He didn't sound like he was bothered either way.

"And you didn't believe me."

"You have no reason to lie."

"No, I don't." But he'd still doubted her. Why was that again? Oh, yes…her father's security reports and his own investigator's report. But still he should have believed her. Shouldn't he?

She tried to catch thoughts that spiraled away as her body's reaction to his nearness began to take precedence. "If I was a virgin, would you be planning to seduce me in cold blood?"

That made him smile, a purely predatory expression that held no comfort for her feminine concerns. "I assure you there will be nothing cold about it."

"Now, you see, I have a hard time understanding how you're going to…" Her brain short-circuited as his hand moved from the back of the couch to her shoulder.

He brushed her collarbone with his thumb. "Yes?"

"Yes?"

His lips hovered above hers. "You were saying?"

"I was saying…" She desperately grasped for reality. "You…I…"

"You…I…what?" he taunted, his voice laced with laughing, masculine triumph.

His amusement sparked her pride and her memory and she pressed her head back into the couch, away from his descending mouth. "I still don't see how you expect to convince me of your passion when you are touching me with the *intent* of convincing me. It's no different than offering a potential client an enhanced guarantee."

The words sounded positively brilliant to her befuddled brain, especially when she considered how many she'd managed to string together.

He looked less than impressed however with her argument. "I can promise you that I do not see you as a client."

She wasn't so sure about that. Now that she'd verbalized the thought, it had taken surprisingly strong root in her mind.

He moved infinitesimally closer. "I want you. Once I have had you, the truth of my desire will be impossible for you to ignore, *pethi mou*."

"You're so darn sure of yourself." She crossed her arm over her small chest and did something totally out of character. She pouted, her lip protruding…the whole bit. And it felt good.

He smiled as if he found her reaction charming and brushed his fingertip down her arm to where it crossed with the other, and then traced the one closest to her body so the back of his fingers made contact with skin bared by her low neckline.

Heat and pleasure rolled over her in a tidal wave of sensation and she gasped.

He stopped with his fingertip in dangerous proximity to her breast. "It is the fact that I am so sure of you that really bothers you, I think."

He was right, darn him. Only she had no time to dwell on that fact because his mouth finished its descent and locked to hers with rock-solid possession. This was no tentative kiss, no prelude to seduction, but the thing itself. In living, glorious color that had starbursts going off inside her and her brain going into a meltdown.

And she went under just as he'd predicted she would. Without a whimper of protest. Without so much as a token attempt to push him away. And she couldn't even claim it was because her hands were trapped between them because he immediately uncrossed her arms for her so that he could get closer with his big, hard body.

She might have been embarrassed if she wasn't enjoying the kiss so much. But nothing had ever felt so right. Well, nothing except his kisses. It had been this way since the very first one. She'd acknowledged then what she knew now. She belonged here, in his arms. Whether he felt a corresponding need, she did not know, but she craved his touch.

Did he sense it? Was that why he was so sure of himself? Of course he did…he was too world savvy not to. But none of that explained why *he* wanted to marry *her*.

CHAPTER FOUR

EVEN THOSE THOUGHTS splintered as his tongue demanded and received entrance into her mouth. His taste intoxicated her and she let him pull her firmly into his body, reveling in the electric charge of contact when her breasts pressed against his chest.

She pulled at his shirt and then scrabbled for buttons, hungry for the feel of his hot skin. They came undone despite the clumsiness of her fumbling fingers and she luxuriated in the silky dark curls that swirled over his chest. He was such a masculine man...everything about him screaming *prime specimen* of the male of their species.

His muscles were granite hard against her exploring fingertips. His sheer size both intimidated and aroused her feminine sensuality.

He made a growling sound in his throat and dragged her into his lap. Planned or not, his desire for her pulsed between them as he had promised it would. She could not deny the harsh reality of his erection pressed against her thigh or the way the hands holding her trembled against her own flesh shimmering with sensation.

But it was so much more than mere physical feeling.

She loved this man and her heart craved this intimate connection as fervently as her body.

His hands slid over the silk of her dress, caressing her curves and inciting feelings that never ceased to shock her. This was what passion was supposed to feel like—not forced, not muted, but so full, so real that every atom in her body shimmered with delight. His hand skimmed up her calf, taking the dress with it and baring her legs to him. He stopped when his fingertips brushed the apex of her thighs through the sheer lace of her panties.

He groaned and pulled his lips from hers. So he could see what he had touched. "Very sexy."

She couldn't form a word to respond. She looked down at herself, sprawled in abandon across his thighs, her legs spread slightly, her thighs quivering with need. She could smell her own musk and rather than embarrass her, it excited her further to think she could respond so totally to this man's kiss.

His bronzed chest gleamed under the muted light cast by the single torchère lamp she'd left on for her return home. His dark body was such a contrast to hers that she was lost in the visual pleasure for long moments.

"I'd like to see you in front of a fireplace, lying naked on a thick rug. Aroused," she said, shocking herself as she admitted one of her favorite nighttime fantasies out loud.

He didn't look taken aback, though; he looked interested. "There is a fireplace in my bedroom. After we are married, I will be very pleased to see that you get your wish."

"I haven't said I'll marry you." Where the wit to say so came from, she didn't know, but she suspected that self-preservation was as instinctual as sexual intimacy.

"You will."

"Maybe."

He chose that moment to slide his finger up and down along the edge of the scrap of fabric that covered her feminine center. She moaned and arched toward his touch, wanting him to move his finger just a fraction of an inch to the left.

He repeated the caress, his expression feral. "I will convince you."

"You can try," she invited, one hand diving to cup the hardness that proved his desire was every bit as real as hers.

She was not a bold lover, but it was imperative for her newly discovered feelings to make him acknowledge, if only tacitly, that this was far from one-sided.

He gasped and then cursed and it was her turn to smile.

Pleasure zinged through her at his response. Perhaps her lack of boldness in the past was because her single sexual liaison had occurred when she was barely nineteen. Her previous lover had been older and a whole lot more experienced than she.

As Sandor's touch ignited raging fires of need inside her, Ellie realized her former lover might have known more, but he had not been particularly good at lovemaking. And that knowledge took away some of the lingering sting the memories had on her emotions. If that man had been as good at evoking a response as Sandor, she would never have escaped the relationship relatively unscathed. She might not have escaped at all, despite what she'd learned back then.

At the time, she'd thought her heart was decimated by his calculation and betrayal, but five years on, she had to admit that it could have been so much worse. That truth served as a chilling reminder for the present, bringing her back to reality with a vicious jerk to her emotions. Because this *was* Sandor. She *did* love him and his potential to hurt her was beyond anything she'd ever known.

Terror coursed through her, cooling blood heated by wanton desire.

She'd learned to expect less from her dad, but would she ever be able to affect the emotional distance necessary to accept that kind of relationship with Sandor? She didn't want to, even if she could. She didn't want a half-life in her marriage. She wanted something fully vibrant between them. But was that a fool's dream?

"What is the matter?" He was looking at her face now, his expression marred by a slight frown.

She blinked and stared at him realizing he'd stopped touching her completely. "Nothing."

But it was a lie. Worries were pounding inside her mind with painful frequency and power. He could hurt her. So much. Was letting him make love to her the smartest thing she could do? Did she want to give him a bigger hold on her heart than he already had?

He wanted to marry her, the side of her brain that housed her libido reminded her with strident urgency. He wasn't going to leave her in the dust. But her first lover had wanted to marry her, too. Only his reasons hadn't been what he'd said they were, or what she needed them to be. Love had not even been a minor variable in the equation.

"You were thinking of something else," Sandor said, not willing to let it drop.

"And that bothers you?"

"Considering what we are doing. Yes."

"Ah, male ego. No need for yours to get dented. I was thinking about you." The words this time were *more* sarcastic than she intended, but she felt powerless to change her tone.

His dark brows drew together, but he did not pull

away. "Right now, I want you being *with* me…thinking only of *this*."

She wasn't expecting another assault to her senses so quickly. Probably because her thoughts and feelings were so divergent, she expected his to be impacted as well. But Sandor knew what he wanted and he went for it.

This was a kiss so carnal, it shattered her fears and her ability to think, leaving her reeling in a maelstrom of need she could not navigate. This was touching and caressing that left her mindless with need and so incoherent she didn't even realize she had been undressed until she was naked and being carried to her bedroom in Sandor's strong arms. She must have done some clothing removal herself because his torso was fully exposed and his bare feet slapped against the hardwood floors of her apartment.

Her body burned with the need to fuse with his and she pressed against him as if she could achieve it in that position.

"Yes, go wild for me, Eleanor. You are everything a man could wish for."

"Ellie," she gasped, needing him to call her by the name she preferred, the one that in her mind fit the true woman she was. This was too intimate for the formal name no one but her father used anymore.

Dark eyes glittered into hers. "Ellie." Then he said a short Greek word that carried a wealth of meaning. *Mine*.

He was claiming her and right that second she could not gainsay him. She needed him more than the air she breathed…she did belong to him. At least for tonight.

Pressing feverish kisses along his collarbone, up his neck and along his jaw, she refused to think. She could only feel. Emotions deep inside, physical pleasure along every nerve ending, joy and purpose radiating off of Sandor. It all mixed together in a combustible package that rocked her to her very soul. She had been born for this moment and she would revel in its splendor.

"Sandor…" She licked under his jaw.

He growled and fell on the bed with her. She landed in a sprawl on top of him, but he quickly flipped her over and took her mouth. She opened her lips, inviting his tongue and deepening the kiss. He rubbed his lower body against hers and she went rigid with shock at the pleasure.

He'd gotten rid of his pants with the rest of his clothes and his erection was touching a place no one else had gotten near in five years. It felt amazing. He was rock-hard and yet the skin was soft and felt totally delicious pressing against her most feminine place.

He yanked his head back. "You are ready for me."

"Yes!" She tried to wriggle to invite him in.

He wouldn't let her move. "Protection?" he gritted.

For a brain totally fuzzed by sexual desire, hers worked quickly to figure out what he needed and the answer to that need. "Drawer by the bed."

She'd bought the condoms when they started dating, assuming he would press for intimacy. There was enough of her brain functioning to appreciate his re-membering to ask.

He wanted her to marry him, but he wasn't going to try to trap her with pregnancy. Warmth unfurled inside her at the knowledge. Her other lover had not been so noble. She thanked God that his ignoble intentions had born no fruit, but she'd never forget the sense of betrayal when she realized what he'd tried to do.

Sandor reared off of her and rushed to the nightstand, ripped open the drawer and then grabbed a condom from the box with flattering speed. He rolled it on and then climbed back on the bed and stalked toward her on his knees. It felt just like a predator was preparing to leap at his prey. A surprisingly pleasurable atavistic shiver shook her frame at the knowledge she was that prey.

He cupped her small breast and kneaded it, sending delirious enjoyment arcing through her. She moaned.

He whispered in her ear, "Your desire for me is real, as is mine for you."

"Yes."

"The passion, it is here between us," he said in a thick Greek accent. "It is real."

"Yes," she repeated.

"Believe," he said and then kissed her again.

She wasn't sure what he meant, but she accepted his mouth and his touch, freely returning both. When he moved on top of her, she spread her thighs in blatant instinctive invitation. He maneuvered his shaft so it pressed against her silky, wet opening.

He stopped. Stopped moving. Stopped kissing her. Even stopped making those sexy male noises of pleasure that had been emitting from his throat.

Her eyes fluttered open and met a dark gaze intent on her.

"Do you accept me into your body?" he asked.

He had to know she wanted him, so this question meant something more, but she wasn't sure what. Only it didn't matter. Her answer was, "Yes."

He nodded as if sealing a pact and then pushed inside her.

Silken tissues stretched and her body absorbed him as if they had been created to fit together perfectly. She felt filled to capacity, yet instead of hurting…it felt good. Really, really good.

Feminine fear that had nothing to do with wanting to stop fluttered through her, but it did not decrease her arousal. It increased it, making her crave movement and total possession. "I want all of you."

"Can you take all of me?"

"I was made to." She wasn't sure what she was saying, but it felt right.

He rocked his pelvis forward, sliding further into her humid depths. Continuing the motion, he took her body slow inch by slow inch until his pelvic bone pressed against hers. Both sensations made her gasp.

He said something in Greek she didn't get.

She luxuriated in the feeling of oneness for a timeless moment. "I told you we would fit."

He husked a laugh. "Usually it is the man comforting the woman with that line."

"Is it?" she asked, not knowing and caring very little what the norm was between other men and women.

She knew only what was right between them and this was right. She tried to arch against him. "I need you to move."

And he did. So perfectly that tears washed into her eyes and leaked down her temples. He seemed to understand because he sipped at them and continued to make love to her as her body built toward a cataclysm of pleasure that was unlike anything she'd ever known.

Then something happened that was surely a miracle because his body went tense above hers at the same moment that she felt the explosion inside. He shouted. She cried out. And their bodies shuddered together in mutual abandon. He continued to move in small, caressing motions that drew the pleasure out for both of them.

Her body jerked with spasms of release while he

groaned and bucked against her a few more times before collapsing on top of her in a heavy, but welcome heap.

His breath bellowed in her ear and her chest labored to draw air in. "That was amazing," she whispered, afraid of ruining the perfect moment with too much sound.

"Yes, it was," he rumbled against her neck, sending shivers along her oversensitive skin.

She turned her head and kissed the side of his face. "Thank you."

"The pleasure was as much or more mine."

"I'm glad you didn't say all yours."

"It would not be true."

She laughed softly at his arrogance, but fell silent quickly. He was so right. It would not be true. She'd never felt anything so wonderful. And she wanted to feel this again. And again. And again.

Which was why he had made love to her, wasn't it? To convince her that they were meant for each other. If not in love, in lust and in like.

"I am going to adore having you as my wife in my bed," he said, confirming his thoughts ran parallel in content if not intent to hers.

"That is not a done deal, yet, Sandor."

He leaned back to fix her with his "get serious" look. She'd seen it a few times before, but it was funny in their current situation and she couldn't help laughing again.

"I do not find this funny. You will marry me, Ellie."

At least he got the name right. She stifled her laughter and cupped his cheek. "Making love with you was incredible, but I still need time to think."

"After what we have just experienced together, how can you need time to think?"

"Because we won't spend our entire life in bed, Sandor."

"It is worth considering."

She shook her head. "You're such a man."

"I am that." He carefully rolled off of her and padded naked to the bathroom. "I would be little use to you in this situation if I wasn't," he called back over his shoulder.

She couldn't argue that logic and did not even try.

He stayed the night and made love to her again in the wee hours of the morning and then again when they awoke to her alarm. Both times left her a boneless, quivering mass of satisfaction. But he did not push again for a definitive answer from her. It was as if he was so sure of her, he was simply biding his time.

She didn't really care why he refrained from pressing her, but was merely glad that he did. He left her house after a brief shower to go home and change for work, while she rushed through her morning routine in order not to be late herself.

There was no time to think or try to decide what the night before had meant.

He called her later that morning, but she was with a client and didn't get a chance to call him back until midway through what should have been her lunch hour.

"I had hoped we could share lunch, *pethi mou*, but I see that idea is a washout."

She looked at the case files dumped on her desk that morning by another counselor before going home ill and sighed. "Unfortunately, yes it is."

"Dinner tonight? Mama hopes to see you."

If he hadn't phrased it like that, she might have said no. She needed some time to get her head together and it wasn't going to happen during work hours filled with the overbooked caseloads of both herself and her absent co-worker. But she liked Hera Christofides. A lot.

And Ellie had no intention of hurting the very sweet older woman's feelings. "I'd love to. What time would you like me to arrive?"

"I will pick you up at six."

"I'd rather drive myself."

"I prefer to see to your comfort."

"You know I'm followed by a security team. I'll be perfectly safe driving myself to your house and home again."

"Nevertheless, I would rather drive you. It is the male prerogative."

"In a former decade maybe."

"Some traditions are best not left behind. Besides, it has not escaped my notice that you do not like to drive."

He was speaking the truth. She didn't. She hated negotiating city traffic and would prefer to ride public transport to work, but with her "secret" security detail following her every move, that wasn't an option. She could accept her dad's offer of a car and chauffer, but something seemed wrong about showing up for a public service job that way. And she wasn't a wimp.

She could drive, she just didn't like to. And Sandor had noticed.

"You're going to be stubborn about this, aren't you?" she asked, but there was no ire in her voice.

She was too busy feeling cherished. She should probably tell him thank you, but she didn't want to feed his already overly certain belief that he always knew what was best.

"Can you doubt it?"

She laughed softly. "Not when stubborn is the thing you do best."

"I would say after last night that you would consider I had at least one or two other attributes."

Despite the fact that no one else could hear his words, she blushed a hot crimson. "Sandor!"

He laughed, the sound low and sexy, affecting her in ways she tried to ignore. The fiend.

She waited for him to stop laughing and then said by way of dismissal, "I'll see you at six."

"I shall look forward to it."

She hung up the phone feeling just slightly outmaneuvered, but she didn't really mind. One of the problems she'd had dating was that after growing up around her father and having to push so hard against him for any sort of independence, most other men seemed a little too easily led in comparison. At first, she'd thought that was what she wanted.

She didn't want to be used again and she didn't want to be dominated, so she very selectively dated men that were from her world and weren't looking for her father's millions to support them, but who were also patently non-aggressive. Men who spouted feminist ideals better than she did and who were sensitive. Men who did not have Sandor's vibrancy or personal power.

She'd grown weary of the dating scene quickly and it wasn't until Sandor bulldozed into her life that she realized what was missing. She wanted a man of integrity, but not one she could lead around by a ring through his nose. She wouldn't tolerate being dominated, and if he didn't already know that, he would learn, but she was glad he was so strong.

She'd learned that a man could be aggressive and powerful and sensitive to her feelings. At least some of them. Which was more than she'd ever had, but not the same as having his love. However, Sandor was always careful to look after her. His recognition of her dislike of driving was not an isolated incident. He watched her. He paid attention.

And that was very different from her father. Which considering how many similarities she saw between the two of them was a very good thing.

Added to that, she didn't live in fear of denting his fragile male ego because he wasn't *overly* sensitive. The fact her father approved was a double-edged sword. His lack of emotional connection to her had resulted in a sense of rebellion toward all that he stood for. But there was a tiny part of her that still wanted his approval. That still hoped deep inside that if she could please him enough, he would love her like a daddy was supposed to love his little girl.

Marrying Sandor would definitely please her father, but his similarity to the man who had lacerated Ellie's heart time and again with twenty-four years of almost complete indifference gave her pause. How could it do anything else?

She couldn't live the rest of her life in that same emotional wasteland with a husband. Even if *she* loved *him.*

Her disturbing thoughts were interrupted by a phone call and she didn't have another second to call her own for the rest of the day. She left work late and had to rush through getting ready for dinner at the Christofides home.

Sandor asked about her day when he picked her up and spent the entire drive to his home listening. It was a heady experience, being the central focus of his attention. With pleasure, she ticked a mental mark on his scorecard…on the side that said, "Not a carbon copy of George Wentworth."

He helped her from the car and she stayed him with a hand, reaching up to kiss him on the corner of his mouth. "Thank you."

His brows drew together. "For what?"

"For listening. I can't imagine that my attempts to help my clients better their lives is all that fascinating, but you never tell me to shut up."

He leaned down and kissed her full on the lips. "You are wrong."

She was clinging to his biceps for support after the short but devastating kiss. "About what?"

"Everything about you interests me, but your desire to help others is both admirable and yes, fascinating to me."

"You're a special man, Sandor." But was it true? If everything about her interested him, why was he so ignorant about some basic elements to her nature? Most important being her need for an emotional connection with him.

"Remember that."

"It's not something I could forget."

He just smiled and led her into the house.

CHAPTER FIVE

HERA CHRISTOFIDES WAS every bit as pleased to see Ellie as Sandor had said she would be and made her welcome with warm effusiveness.

"It is so good you come. Sandor, he is like a caged lion lately, but when you are here…he is better." She squeezed Ellie's hand before taking a seat on the large white sofa and indicating Ellie should join her.

"Mama, I do not mind being likened to a lion, but I am far from caged."

"There are many kinds of cages, my son," Hera said wisely. "Though I agree, you are very like a lion in the cage or out of it…because you see the world as your prey." She sighed, her eyes so like Sandor's filled with concern. "It is always the business with you. You want to win, win, win."

Sandor shrugged. "Better that than I be a lazy layabout, no?" His speech pattern always took on a more decidedly Greek bent when he was around his mother.

Hera pursed her lips and appealed to Ellie with her eyes. "I cannot imagine this one lazy. Can you?"

Ellie shook her head solemnly, though a smile flirted at the edges of her mouth. "No. I really can't."

"There, you see?" Hera said as if making a point.

Though Ellie had to wonder if Sandor knew what it was supposed to be because she wasn't sure she did. She smiled regardless.

"And what am I supposed to see, Mama?" Sandor asked.

"That to work all the time is its own cage," the older woman said, as if it should be obvious.

"Better that cage than many others I could name."

"Perhaps, but it would be better not to be caged at all. Do you not agree, Eleanor?"

"Yes. Freedom is a beautiful thing and something we often have to sacrifice other things to attain."

"Ah, this one, she is smart. You hold on to her, son." Hera patted Ellie's arm.

Sandor smiled. "I intend to, believe me."

Hera nodded. "Good."

Thankfully that was all she and Sandor said on the subject and Ellie had to be grateful that he had not told his mother he had asked Ellie to marry him. She had a feeling Hera wouldn't be above trying to convince Ellie she should say yes.

So, why hadn't Sandor pulled his mother in to argue his case? It seemed like a tactic he would use.

On the other hand, she'd asked for time to think and apparently Sandor intended to respect that. Which was a pretty darn effective argument in his favor, if he but knew it.

Since she wasn't pressuring Ellie to accept her beloved son's proposal, having Hera there as a buffer made the evening more relaxing. But nothing could mitigate the fact that Ellie's mind insisted on playing the events of the night before over and over in her head. Being slammed at work had helped to keep her thoughts under control, but being in his company made it impossible to keep the memories at bay.

She would catch Sandor looking at her like a shark ready

to gobble her up and she would stammer and blush and in general react without her usual aplomb. His mother would take him to task for embarrassing her and Sandor would just grin, pleading innocence if not ignorance.

An important call came in during dessert and Sandor excused himself to take it in his study.

Hera shook her head after he left. "He puts too much importance on business, that one. I thought bringing him to America would give him a better life. It is not so easy to be a child without a father in a small village like the one we came from, but now I wonder if I made the right choice. Had we stayed there, he would not be so driven by business maybe."

"I don't believe Sandor is the kind of man to be defined by his surroundings. He is who he is and would be that man, no matter where he'd spent the last years of his childhood. It wouldn't have mattered if he started in a small town in Greece instead of Boston, your son would have climbed his way to the top no matter what. I think if you'd stayed there, though, that it would have taken longer and been harder for him. He might not be where he is right now, but never doubt he would have achieved what he set out to achieve."

"Thank you, Eleanor. You are a kind and very percep-tive young woman."

The praise filled Ellie with a sense of well-being, of be-longing. She grinned. "And just think, if he had to work harder to get where he is, he would have taken longer to begin considering matters besides business."

She wasn't about to spill the beans about his proposal, but she figured Hera was savvy enough to realize her son's thoughts had turned to domestic matters.

The older woman's expression turned-horror struck.

"You think he might have made me wait even longer to get grandbabies?"

Ellie laughed. She knew the other woman was intuitive where her son was concerned. "I'm afraid so."

Hera shook her head again. "I still worry about him. He never stops achieving. When is it enough?"

"He seems to have things to prove to himself," Ellie said carefully.

This time Hera's sigh carried a wealth of sadness. "Yes. He wishes to prove he got nothing bad from his father. My papa, he was a good man, but he was hard. He made Sandor to think he was responsible for things that he had no control over. Papa said nothing good about the young boy I loved, but he was good. Too young to be as strong as he needed to be maybe, but he *was* good."

"Do you ever tell Sandor that?"

"I tried, but while Papa lived, it would have been disrespectful to say his words were not all truth. By the time he died, his beliefs were settled so deeply inside Sandor, I could not sway them. And part of me…I blamed Jimmy for never coming back. There were things I did not know at the time. I now regret never speaking against my father's words."

Ellie reached out and touched Hera's arm. "It must have been hard for you."

"It was. I was raised to be a good girl…to hold my innocence for marriage, but the love I had with Sandor's father…it was overwhelming. I have never known anything like it since. You will think me a fool, but he has always been the husband of my heart."

"I don't think it is foolish at all. I've heard of love like that." And for the first time, she wondered if she really wanted feelings that deep with a man.

That kind of love had always been her idyll, but now, seeing Hera's pain, the hurt in those beautiful brown eyes so fresh it could have happened yesterday, Ellie's own heart twinged with both sympathy and fear. Compassion for the other woman filled her along with a terror that Ellie's own feelings were already as at risk as Hera's had been.

She was no naïve sixteen-year-old with her first lover, but she had a suspicion that the kind of love Hera was talking about transcended age and even experience.

Hera's smile wiped the pain from her eyes as they glowed with a remembered feeling so powerful it could still bring her joy as well as hurt. "To feel it is beyond any other riches this world has to offer. To have it returned, a gift of unimaginable pleasure. We both felt it. He loved me as much as I loved him."

"Yet he left." Ellie didn't say it because she doubted Hera, but because she could not understand walking away from something so special. Still, belatedly, she realized, she should not have said the words aloud. "I'm sorry. I should not have said that."

"Why not? It is the truth. But only part of the truth. Papa caught us together and he beat my love until he could not get up." Tears filled Hera's eyes. "I tried to stop him, but Papa slapped me hard and Jimmy told me to leave. He could not stand for me to be hurt. I would not listen to my papa, but I listened to Jimmy. It wounded his pride for me to see him beaten like that also, I could tell. He would not raise his hand to my father, so he had no defense. Papa thought it was his right to do what he did, but he drove Jimmy off the island."

"So, he didn't leave you voluntarily?"

"No. He had no way of knowing I had become pregnant.

He was only a teenager himself. A young boy on holiday with his friends. He tried to see me once after that."

Ellie's insides clenched. Did Sandor know that?

"I did not know he had done so until after Papa's death. I found the letter in his bureau. At first, I did not tell Sandor because he was already grieving the loss of his grandfather, but later…I did not know what purpose it would serve. It had been so long and I had convinced myself Jimmy had married and had more children. Sandor already struggled with so much, to expose him to such a situation would have hurt him even more I thought. And he was bitter toward his father. I thought to wait would be best."

"You were probably right."

Hera's eyes filled with doubt. "I wonder. I never married. I had opportunity, but I had no desire. Was it the same for my Jimmy? I had to choose between using the money I got from selling my family home and possessions for Sandor's schooling or to search out his father. I made my choice, but I often wonder if it was the right one."

"But now that you have the money, you could find him."

"I broached the subject with Sandor once. I learned to regret it. Had I not asked, I could have done so without repercussion, but because I told him what I wanted to do, he asked me not to use money from his hard work to find a man who had abandoned us both. I could not change his mind."

"Did you tell him that his father wrote?"

"It did not matter to him."

"Sandor is very stubborn."

"Yes."

Said stubborn man returned soon thereafter, but Ellie could not get her discussion with Hera out of her mind.

When he took her home, he once again parked in the

visitor parking garage and asked to come up. She knew what was coming, but she wanted to talk to him about what Hera had told her and if she was honest with herself (and she had a policy of being scrupulously so) she wanted what he wanted. Very much.

This time, she went directly to the kitchen and put the kettle on for tea.

"I am not thirsty," he said from behind her.

"I want tea." *And time to talk*, she added silently.

His dark brow rose, but he bowed slightly. "Then we shall have tea."

"You're making fun of me."

"I am humoring you. It is not the same."

"I see. Why are you humoring me?"

"For obvious male reasons. I hope to sweeten your temperament toward me so that I may have my wicked way with you."

She laughed. "I think you know you can seduce me without a pot of tea first."

"But I prefer not to seduce."

"You want me to offer myself?"

"Is that so bad?"

She shrugged. She didn't suppose it was, but she frowned anyway. "You think indulging before bed will make me more inclined to invite you to share mine?"

"I will do my best to convince you."

"I thought you weren't out to seduce me."

"Reminding you of the pleasure we shared last night is hardly a seduction."

Right. "And that's your plan, to remind me?"

"And entice you with thoughts of what tonight could bring."

Luckily for her already heating libido, the teakettle whistled and she jumped into action, making a pot of herbal tea that would not keep either of them awake. Though she had a feeling Sandor would effectively do so anyway.

They were sitting at her small 1950s restored yellow Formica kitchen table when she broached the subject of his dad. "Have you ever considered finding your father?"

Sandor's body tensed. "I suppose it was too much to expect that my time on the phone would not provide the opportunity for Mama to open this particular can of worms tonight. What happened, did she drag out the sorry tale of how my grandfather beat James Foster and chased him away?"

"You're uncannily prescient." She grinned teasingly, wanting to keep it light, but not sure that was going to be a possibility with the look on his face. "I don't suppose you were eavesdropping?"

He sighed and drank his tea. "No, but it's a story she's tried to feed me more than once."

"It's not a story. Your mother wouldn't make something like that up."

"I have no doubt my grandfather did as she said, but what does that change? My father was too weak to return for her. That is the bottom line."

"He tried."

"She told you about the letter, too?" Sandor sounded pained.

"Yes."

"Look, I read that letter and it was hardly the missive of a love pining away for her company. He had finished university, he thought they could see each other again…for old time's sake. He said nothing of the love she insists they both felt so strongly. He said something about thinking she might have married by now because Greek girls married younger than American ones, or some such rot."

"Did you think he should have poured his heart out in a letter to a woman he couldn't even be sure wasn't married?"

"If his love was as great as my mother claimed, he would have." Sandor's tone was hard, brooking no argument.

She gave it anyway. "Would *you* have?"

"I do not believe in that kind of love."

"Yes, I know, but even if you did, I don't believe you would put your heart on the line until you knew the lay of the land."

That seemed to take him back a little. "What is the point of this conversation?"

"I think you should find your father, if not for your sake, then for hers."

Sandor pushed his tea away and leaned back in his chair, the caged lion coming to mind again. "You think I do not take her feelings into account when I refuse to seek him out?"

"Do you?"

"Yes." He rubbed his hand over his face as if tired all of a sudden. "Tell me, what do you think it would do to my tenderhearted mother to discover my father married soon after graduation and has other children and a wife he adores?"

"Does he?" Had Sandor had the man investigated?

"I do not know and that is the point. In this instance, ignorance is bliss. At least as far as my mother is concerned."

"But if he is married, you would not have to tell her about him."

"I would not...could not lie to Mama."

"But is a lie of omission always a lie, if you are just protecting her? Wouldn't it be better for you to know?"

Sandor shrugged. "I love my mother. To withhold that

information from her if I had it would be wrong. It would breach the trust we have between us. I won't risk her being further hurt."

Wow. How could she help loving this man?

"But what if you are wrong?"

"Then he would have come for her in all this time."

It was a telling argument. "What about you? Don't you want to know him?"

"He deserted my mother, he abandoned me though he did not know about me. He is not a man I want in my life."

"Your grandfather kept them apart."

"There was only one letter, Ellie, not ten, not five, not even two. Just one. He struck out on the first swing and never picked up the bat again."

"You can't imagine doing that, can you?"

"No. Not when it pertains to something important to me."

"I'm stubborn, too, you know."

"We have established that, yes."

"I believe you are wrong."

"I believe I would rather discuss the way your nipples taste and how they harden and swell against my tongue."

Shocked, her mouth opened on a gasp, but no other sound came out. Under the bright, fluorescent lights in the kitchen, the look he gave her was hot and wicked. It seemed so out of place in the cheery room and yet…not. This man and his earthy sensuality fit into her life in surprisingly adept ways.

Because as startling as his unrefined words had been, they had also aroused her. She licked her lips, tasting tea and the honey she'd used to sweeten it. "That's not something a person usually discusses."

"But I like telling you how sweet you taste, how good you feel inside my mouth."

Her breath stilled somewhere between inhaling and exhaling. "You can be very…basic."

He leaned forward and brushed the back of his knuckles over one—yes, very erect—nipple.

She moaned.

He smiled, a man who clearly liked the impact he had on her. "I think despite your prim public image, primitive excites you. You like to hear these words from me."

He was right, but no other man she'd ever known would have considered saying such a thing, not to make the first comment, much less *tell her that she liked it*. For goodness' sake. Sandor was so different. Was that why she was drawn to him?

He defied the molds life would say he had to fit inside…just as she tried to. Or thought she did.

"You think I'm prim?" She looked down at the simple Albert Nipon suit in oyster shell silk she'd chosen to wear to dinner with his mother. Though its chic styling was form-fitting, it wasn't exactly sexy. The jacket buttoned up as a top showed nothing of her unimpressive cleavage and the skirt stopped modestly just shy of her knees. "Do you think I dress too conservatively?"

"The way you dress is perfect for you, Ellie. I like knowing that the rest of the world looks at you and sees what appears to be a coolly elegant woman, but I know that under the prim facade is a body made just for mine that responds with an uninhibited passion that delights me." His knuckles continued to brush up and down over her sensitized nub. "And sometimes you dress more provocatively than I think you intend to."

"You don't believe I *intend* to provoke you?" She could barely breathe, much less think with the way he touched her and the sensual timber of her voice saying such intensely erotic things just for her.

"I do not believe you have any idea how very sexy I find both the prim little suits or clothing like the dress you had on last night."

She'd wanted to be sexy the night before. It *had* been on purpose, but he didn't know that? "Why do you say that?"

"If you did, you would never have questioned the passion between us."

A man's brain was certainly a mysterious puzzle, especially Sandor's. "Was I supposed to read your mind?"

He shrugged. "I hope you now have a better basis to draw your conclusions from."

"I suppose I do." She grabbed his wrist, stopping that tantalizing touch that was melting her brain and other body parts. "I felt the passion in you before…leashed," she got out, "but I doubted my instincts when you did nothing to act on it."

"And now?"

She took a deep breath, but it didn't help get her senses under control. Her breasts felt full inside the lacy cups of her bra and the breath actually made them move against the silky fabric, arousing her further. She bit back a moan and closed her eyes, trying to find her control in blackness behind her lids. "Now I concede that we are very good together that way."

If only she knew whether, or not, he was that good with every other woman he'd been with. She knew how special it was for her, but what about him?

For her, last night…even right now…was a totally unique experience, but maybe he always found that much satisfaction in the act of lovemaking. She wanted to believe otherwise, but deceiving herself as to the meaning of sex with a man had broken her heart once before. She refused to do that to herself again.

He stood up from the table and came around to lift her to her feet. She was so close to his body, she could feel his heat, but they were not quite touching except where his big hands cupped her elbows. Her eyes opened of their own accord, taking in his heated brown gaze.

He caressed the sensitive area of her inner elbow with both thumbs. "Let us go be good together again, hmm?"

"So we are done talking about your father?"

"Yes." He cupped her face, tilting her chin with his thumbs. "We are done talking at all, I think."

"I suppose I can live with that," she husked. Her body was clamoring for his touch, but she fought the urge to press into him.

She wanted to play it cool, not to give too much of herself away. But that hope disintegrated with the first brush of his lips against hers. The brief contact zinged through her like an overload of electric current, making her body jolt and stiffen and her lips part and beg silently for more.

He gave it to her, covering her mouth with his completely, taking possession and yet inviting her to share in it…to make it mutual. And she wanted that, too. She needed to know that she was branding him as hers as effectively as he had marked her as his. He accepted the tentative slide of her tongue and invited her to go further. It was amazing.

Where had he learned to make love so completely with nothing more than lips against lips? Or had he been born with the ability? Sandor was a special man, part of her insisted it had to be inherent to him. The other part of her tried very hard not to be jealous of the women who had come before.

He kissed down along her neck and she shivered. "Sandor?"

"Hmmm?" He nibbled at a particularly sensitive spot, making her whole body shake with reaction.

"You know the whole don't have sex with virgins unless you're married to them or very close to it thing you've got going in your brain?" She wasn't sure where the words came from or the ability to speak coherently enough to voice them, but they came from that part of her brain that was not properly protected when he touched her.

The vulnerable part.

He laughed against her collarbone. "Ellie *mou,* how do you have the wherewithal to ask me questions? I must be doing something wrong."

"No." She panted a little as his tongue darted out to taste the hollow of her neck. "That's the point. You do this so well. I just wondered?"

"What?"

"How did you learn all this stuff? You're so good at it."

He groaned and buried his mouth against her. "You taste so good. I cannot believe you asked me that."

"It's just…I couldn't decide if your grandfather and you thought it was okay for you to have sex with women who are experienced. That seems like such a double standard, and then of course, there's *your* virginity to consider."

"I assure you, I am not a virgin."

"But didn't it bother you having sex when you were? You know the first time. Or did the woman plan to marry you and something go wrong?" The thought of him engaged to another woman was not a comfortable one.

His body shook with laughter even as his mouth kept doing truly decadent and delicious things to her. "You are right. I am guilty of a double standard."

"Explain it to me."

"There are women who are open to sex without commitment."

"Yes." That was true.

"You are not one of them."

"But I'm not a virgin."

"Yet, you are still very innocent."

That wasn't something she wanted to dwell on, but compared to him…maybe. "So, you've had sex with lots of women?"

He sighed and straightened so their eyes met. "Not lots. I am no playboy."

"But you know so much…you like it a lot." He'd been really attentive the night before. Hungry even. "I can't see you celibate."

"Then your imagination has let you down, though mine could not conceive of this conversation. So, perhaps we are even. Only consider that for years I worked twenty-hour workdays and took only the breaks my mother demanded I give her. Neither instance is conducive to ongoing sexual liaisons."

"But you have had lovers?"

"I have had sex partners. Even when the same woman met that need for more than a few nights, the relationship would never be something I would describe as lovers. Or even a relationship really. We scratched a mutual itch."

"That sounds so cold." And crude, but she was getting used to his earthy way of discussing certain things.

He had not been raised in the refined and often stifling atmosphere she had been subjected to.

"It was. I did not realize how cold until I warmed at the fire of your honest passion the first time we kissed."

CHAPTER SIX

WETNESS BURNED BEHIND her eyes, her emotions choking her. He might not believe in love, but that sounded like she was special to him. She said so.

"Of course you are special. I want to marry you. You are my lover and you will one day be my wife."

She didn't have the strength to deny him right then—wasn't even sure she wanted to, so she avoided answering altogether by kissing him. He growled and yanked her body into his, pressing his hardness against her in a blatant demand and claim at the same time. She had no intention of refusing that demand, no hope to do so even if she'd wanted to.

He swept her into his arms and carried her into the bedroom, laying her down on the bed carefully as if she were both fragile and precious. She looked up at him, her heart in her eyes, her teeth clamped together to bite back the words of love that wanted to tremble from her lips.

He stood and began to undress. "Tonight, I want to take it very slow."

Her body was already suffused with heat and longing and they'd barely done anything. "I don't think I'll survive slow."

"You will more than survive it, you will enjoy it." His husky laugh warmed her. "I guarantee it."

"You're very confident."

"According to you, I have reason to be. You like my lovemaking. You think I am so good at it, you wonder how I learned such skill." Oh, he sounded arrogant, but pleased, too, and she couldn't help smiling.

"Yes, well…"

He smiled, taking those two words as wholehearted agreement. "There you see?"

But she was beyond answering. He was peeling off his shirt and revealing bronze skin covered with silky black hair over sculpted muscles that tapered to a narrow waist and an intriguing arrow of hair that hinted at more. He was so incredibly gorgeous and overwhelmingly masculine.

He undid the button on his trousers and she sucked in air. It didn't help her feeling of light-headedness, though.

The man was simply too delicious for words.

He started pushing his trousers down his hips and she thought maybe she should be doing something, too. Though it was hard to move when her body was trembling so hard. She reached for the buttons on the front of her silk jacket.

"Don't," he said with a shake of his head. "I want to undress you."

"You're going to torture me, aren't you?"

"With pleasure….perhaps."

She quaked inside where he could not see. "I'm not going to survive."

"I had not pegged you for such a pessimist."

She laughed, but the sound choked off as he divested himself of his briefs. His erection sprang out from a nest of curly black hair. Even though they'd made love twice the night before and once again that morning, she still felt a frisson of trepidation skitter up her spine at the prospect of taking the big shaft inside her.

"You are looking at me as if I am a snake ready to bite."

She bit her lip. "More like a tree trunk ready to impale."

He laughed out loud, his head going back as amusement shook his tall frame. "You are priceless, Ellie."

Her heart squeezed. To see him like this was so rare and *she* had made it happen. It increased her sense of being special to him.

He was still grinning, looking at her. "You know we fit. Perfectly."

"Yes."

"But you still look nervous."

"I am, a little."

"Let me see what I can do about that." He moved toward the bed and the closer he got the faster her heart sped.

He stopped when his knees pressed against the end of the mattress and reached down to take one of her feet in his hand. He slid the sandal off. "Did you know that there are numerous pleasure points in your feet?"

She shook her head, her throat suddenly too dry to speak.

He cupped her heel in his big palm and used his other hand to massage her arch, sending pleasure arcing through her.

She gasped and moaned, her head falling back against the bed. "I do now."

He chuckled. "You like it?"

Her only answer was a moan as he found one of the pleasure points he'd mentioned. He massaged both feet thoroughly, pressing between her toes and making her squirm with feelings that did not resemble ticklishness in the least. It was both strange and wonderful to have a gorgeous naked Greek caressing her feet while the rest of her body was still fully covered. It was also highly erotic.

Slowly his touch moved up her legs, finding sensitive dips and hollows on her ankles and behind her knees. One spot had her keening his name and arching off the bed.

"You are so beautiful in your passion, Ellie."

"I've never felt like this before," she gasped.

"I am glad."

She was, too. Once again the word special came to her mind, but she still had no idea if what they felt was out of the ordinary for him.

But his fingers had just the slightest tremor as they made their way under her skirt. "Your skin is like satin, so smooth and soft. So perfect, Ellie *mou*."

He massaged her, working his way to her inner thighs and touching flesh that felt as private as her feminine center. In a way it was. No other person touched her thighs like this. She'd never thought about it before, but many parts of her body were actually pretty private and Sandor would touch them all.

He caressed her there, not even slipping a fingertip under the elastic band of her panties and her pleasure grew until she was making little mewling sounds and had spread her legs in silent, begging invitation for more. But he slid his hands back down her legs.

She made a sound of distress and he smiled. "It is time to remove your skirt, I think."

She was more than willing and cooperated by arching off the bed so he could undo the zip and slide it down her hips inch by excruciating inch. It wasn't tight and the lining was smooth so it slid easily, but he was drawing out the unveiling. That's what it felt like. An unveiling.

"You make me feel like you're unwrapping a present, but it's the only one you've got on Christmas morning, so you're taking a long time with it." She could barely speak above a whisper…she could barely speak at all.

"You are a precious gift to me."

The words warmed something deep inside her that had always been cold. That place that needed to be treasured by someone, to know that she held a unique place in someone's heart and life. She'd always thought that if she disappeared from her father's life, he wouldn't even notice. Not really.

But while she might not have a special place in Sandor's heart, he was showing her that he intended her to have a special place in his life. That was better than what she'd had for so long, she almost blurted out her agreement to marry him right there. But some tiny lingering sense of self-preservation stopped her.

Making a decision like this during lovemaking would be stupid. She'd done that once before and she wasn't making that mistake again.

She was panting and ready to rip the rest of her clothes off herself by the time he was done with her skirt, though.

He stayed her hands when she tried. "Not yet. You promised, *pethi mou*."

Had she promised, or simply acquiesced? It didn't matter. She would let him continue because the pleasure was so intense and so was he.

He ran one fingertip along the top edge of her lacy bikini briefs that matched her cream lace bra. "Very nice."

"I don't wear thongs," she said almost apologetically. But she'd worn this particular set with the thought in the back of her mind that as much as she'd known it might not be smart to invite him to her bed a second night in a row, he might end up there anyway.

And here he was.

"These are quite sexy enough." He dipped one finger-tip under the elastic of the waistband. "But I am eager to see you naked."

"Then take them off."

"Not yet."

She pouted for the second time in remembrance.

He pounced, blanketing her body and taking her mouth with a storm of passion that had her arching under him and rubbing the silk clad apex of her thighs against his heated manhood.

He broke the kiss, panting. "You are dangerous, you know that?"

"I like that."

"You are so far from prim, my little Boston princess."

"My wild side only comes out with you."

"As it should be."

It was her turn to laugh. "Your arrogance is showing again."

He shrugged and moved to straddle her thighs so he could start unbuttoning her top. He watched intently as her torso was revealed. She warmed under his gaze, but her own was snagged by the body straddling her. She reached out to touch him, wrapping her fingers around his erection.

The feel of his heated flesh against her hand was so incredible. "It's like satin over steel."

"It feels like steel," he growled.

She smiled and caressed him from top to bottom.

He moaned and she echoed the sound. There was something ferociously arousing about having the freedom to touch him like this. His velvet length jumped in her hand, throbbing against her fingers. But he didn't stop what he was doing.

He made her sit up to remove her suit top and undo the catch on her bra before pulling it off, too. She couldn't help noticing this unveiling had gone much faster than her skirt. Touching him was having its effect.

Naked skin pressed against naked skin and their heat mingled while frissons of sensation sparkled along every point of contact. She squeezed his hardness in reflexive action.

He groaned low and long. "You are dangerous."

"You said that."

"It is true."

"I think we are dangerous together."

He pushed her back onto the bed.

She met his gaze, her own determined. "I want you now, Sandor. No more games."

"This is no game, *pethi mou.*"

And it felt all too serious when one hand cupped her breast, the thumb brushing over her nipple while his other hand clasped her shoulder, holding her body in place as she tried to arch off the bed at the contact.

She moaned, unbearably aroused by his refusal to let her move. She didn't understand why it should be so, or why he felt the need to keep her still. But it didn't matter. Because it was the way it was and it was so intense she could barely stand it.

Her eyelashes fluttered shut and all she could do was feel. Feel his hard thighs straddling her hips. Feel his hands both cupping her breasts now, teasing the rigid tips with his thumbs. She didn't try to move as if they had made a silent agreement for her not to do so. Gently he pinched, then pulled the hard nubs until she wanted to scream.

"Please don't stop," she whispered into the dark void behind her eyelids.

She continued to feel. Feel the pleasure-tension spiraling inside her. Feel her body suffuse with heat and need that grew so big she felt like it would explode out of her before he ever made her his. The scent of their arousal surrounded her as did his personal fragrance.

She could hear her own panting exhalations and his harsh breathing, both sounds like an internal caress that added to the desire coiling tighter and tighter within her. He shifted and the darkness behind her eyelids grew more acute as if she was in his shadow. Then his mouth was on hers—first devouring, then tenderly teasing and then devouring again.

He played on all of her senses, building her to a fever pitch and then drawing her back again. Repeating the process over and over again, but he was right. It was all much too intense to be called a game.

This man was determined to show her that they fit. That their bodies were perfect complements for each other, or maybe simply that his body could give her more pleasure than any other man would ever be able to.

She had no doubts as she writhed under him.

"Sandor! Please…" But she didn't know what she was pleading for. Completion? Or more of this maddening pleasure?

Sandor's heart contracted at the sound of his name whispered so desperately on Ellie's lips. She was so passionate. So responsive. In every way she fit him. Soon she would understand that truth as well.

He laved the sweet hollow in her throat. "You are so perfect for me, *pethi mou*," he said gutturally.

Her head was twisting on the pillow, but he knew she was not denying him. She was simply beyond the ability to respond verbally. And he had brought her to this state.

Pride surged through him. She had not been a virgin, as she had said she wasn't, but her responses were too over-whelming for her to have ever known what she felt with him with another man. She had said it was different for her, that she had not known this and he believed her.

In this way, he knew he was her first and for no reason he could logically explain, that was very important to him. He had never considered himself a possessive man when it came to his female companions, but then he had never made love to a woman with the intention of claiming her for a lifetime, either.

He moved back off her thighs and removed the last scrap of cloth standing between her and total nudity. No time to draw it out. No will to do so. It was time to claim her. He made quick work of donning protection.

He was pushing her thighs apart, preparing to enter her when he realized he wished to be claimed as well. He did not want mere compliance about this marriage thing. He wanted Ellie to be sure of him. To want more than his body.

For a moment in that bed, the small boy who had with-stood the taunts of other children in his small Greek village because he had no father broke through Sandor's adult armor. He needed to know he belonged.

He looked down at Ellie. "Do you want me inside you?" He stopped moving…stopped touching…and waited.

Her eyes fluttered open. The deep-blue green of the Mediterranean stared at him, shiny and damp with emotion. "Yes, Sandor, only you…inside me."

How did she know those were the words he needed? How had she known to clarify…to use that *only?* That small child inside him, the one who had determined at an age so young he could no longer remember it to be everything others thought he was not—important, powerful, strong—that child knew that Sandor needed that word *only*. His being important to this woman was key to healing wounds he had refused to acknowledge were even there since before they ever left Greece for America.

"You belong to me, Ellie."

"Yes." Her gazed locked with his. "Only you."

He surged inside her, feeling as if for the first time, he had come home. Her body jolted, clenched around him and then she climaxed with a scream as primal as any mating cry. He let her body soak all the joy from that moment it could before he began to move, building the momentum again with thrusts that sealed her as his own.

"Sandor…I can't…it's too much."

He didn't stop, but rotated his pelvis with each thrust. "You can, Ellie. Give me the gift of your pleasure. Come for me, my own."

Her head went back, her heels dug into the mattress and she exploded as he found his own release. His arms barely had the strength to hold his weight off of her and when she tugged him down, he had no reserves to protect her.

She did not seem to mind, but mumbled sweet nothings against his neck, telling him how amazing he was, what an incredible lover, how strong, how perfect. She even told him he was beautiful and while he would never admit it out

loud, he liked hearing all the praise from her sweet mouth.
Even those words.

"I have to take care of the condom," he muttered at
some point.

She smiled, letting her arms slip to the bed and nodded.
"Thank you."

"For what?"

"You know."

"No, I do not."

"For not trying to trap me."

Did she really think him so weak he would resort to
trickery to win his case? He had no need for tricks like that
and with his background, even if he feared she would not
come around otherwise, he would never use them.

Besides, she'd admitted she belonged to him.

When he came back into the bedroom after washing up,
she was snuggled under the covers, barely conscious. She
made no demur when he climbed into bed beside her.

He pulled her into his arms. "You belong to me, Ellie."

"Sandor…"

"Do not deny it." He rolled her onto her back and looked
down at her. "You acknowledged my place in your life
when we made love."

Her blue-green gaze slid away from him, then she
sighed and met his eyes. "I don't deny that my body
belongs to you, but that doesn't mean I'm going to wear
your ring, Sandor."

So much for being barely conscious. She looked ready
to fall asleep any second, but she was thinking clearly
enough to argue.

Frustration roared through him at her words. "What
does it mean then?"

"That I doubt I'll ever let another man into my bed, but I don't know if I can spend the rest of my life with you."

What the hell was that supposed to mean? He sat up and glared down at her, the small light given off by the bedside lamp illuminating an unfathomable feminine expression. "If you will not give yourself to another man, how can you deny my place beside you?"

"I'm not *denying* anything. Please believe me. I'm just not…just not confirming it."

"Semantics."

"No…Sandor…truth. I told you I needed time."

"But after what we have just done—"

Her finger pressed against his lips to silence him. "It was wonderful, Sandor. The most special experience of my life. Please don't ruin it by starting an argument." Her eyes shone with a vulnerability he could not fight.

He nipped her finger gently in retaliation and she pulled it away, but not before he'd laved it with a healing tongue kiss. Still, he growled, "I am not the one arguing here."

Were all women this confusing, or just her? He'd never spent much time trying to understand the workings of the female mind. The only one who had ever mattered enough to him was his mother and that relationship was in no way similar.

Her aqua-blue eyes were filled with feelings he could not identify. "I'm not arguing. I'm scared, Sandor. I don't want to be hurt."

"I will not hurt you."

"But you will. You can't help it." Her eyes drooped as exhaustion overtook her, but the words kept coming as if the thought behind them was so ingrained she did not need to be fully alert to express it. "You don't love me. That is going to cause me pain. I have to decide if it's going to be worse than the pain of letting you go."

He could not believe what he was hearing. "Damn it, I will not hurt you."

"You won't be able to help it." She sounded so sad.

And it made him furious. There was no need. "You tell me what you need and I will make sure you have it." To him, it was that simple. Why could she not see it?

"You can't."

"I can do anything."

Her lips curled in a small, melancholy smile. "I know you believe that, but it's not true. You can't give me the most important thing of all."

"What is so important?"

"Your love."

He felt like he'd been kicked in the chest, but didn't know why. "I can give you everything you need." He knew it was true. "If you want affection, I will give it to you. If you want gifts, I will buy them for you. If you want companionship, it will be yours. There is nothing I will withhold from you."

Her eyes closed, but moisture leaked from the corners and it made him feel helpless, not a sensation he was used to. And certainly not one he liked.

"Except the emotion I've spent my whole life living without." She turned on her side, away from him. "All the things you offer should come from love, but you will give them to me *if I ask*. There's a difference, even if you can't see it. I know that difference intimately."

He put his hand on her shoulder, needing to comfort the raw pain he heard in her voice. "Explain."

Her shoulder rose and fell beneath his hand. "My father

feels responsibility for me, but he doesn't love me. I figured that out when I was little. He's never loved me. Everything he has ever done for me has been out of duty. Now, you are telling me you want to do the same…you will give me what I say I need out of duty as my husband." She turned back to face him and the deeply embedded pain he heard in her voice was in her moisture filled eyes. "There's never been anyone like that for me. No one to love me. No other family after my grandparents died. No long-term friendships to fall back on. Life without love is so lonely, Sandor. I don't want that kind of loneliness in my marriage."

He did not know what to say. He'd always had his mother's love and before his grandfather had died, the old man had loved him, too. In his way. Even so, Sandor had never valued love because he considered it responsible for too much pain.

Ellie was saying the lack of it was just as painful, but she was wrong that it had to be lonely.

"Do you feel lonely now, Ellie?"

She didn't answer, but something in her eyes said she was lonely…deep inside. Even after they had made love so beautifully. He did not understand it. He felt more connected to her than he had to any other person. How could she not feel the connection?

"I don't want to spend the rest of my life waiting for the people I love to love me back," she said into the silence between them.

"Are you saying you love me, Ellie?"

The moisture in her eyes overflowed, tracking down her cheeks in a stream of tears and she whispered, "Yes."

Had he considered it two days ago, he would have said that her falling in love with him would help him convince her to marry him, but now he knew it was far more likely to cause her to turn her back on what they could have. She was genuinely afraid of being hurt by him. Because he did not love her.

Something squeezed inside him, making it hard to breathe. He knew what it was to hurt. As impossible as it should be, he was hurting right now. For her. But also for himself.

Her uncertainty was tearing at old wounds. Memories best forgotten, but that haunted him all the same. He had spent his childhood rejected for what he was. The illegitimate son of a Greek woman and her American lover. The best in sports and academics, his schoolmates and even his teachers had still looked at him as if he did not measure up because he did not share his father's last name.

No amount of effort on his part could force their full acceptance, or his grandfather's unconditional approval. And he could not force Ellie to accept him, either. He did not want to even try. She deserved to come to terms with their relationship on her own, but he also needed to know that the choice had been completely hers.

Would her love be like his grandfather's, tempered by expectations and needs Sandor had little hope of fulfilling? Or would it be like his mother's love…unconditional and willing to accept him for who he was? He was self-aware enough to realize that while he did not need her love, if he had it, he wanted it to come with acceptance.

He said nothing in response to her declaration. He did not know what to say that would not hurt her further. He could not return the words in all honesty and it seemed wrong to thank her for something he was not sure would not end up hurting him as love so often did.

So, he kissed her instead. Gentle, coaxing kisses that lasted until she stopped crying and slipped into sleep, her arms wrapped tightly around him, her head resting on his shoulder.

CHAPTER SEVEN

ELLIE SAT ON THE BEACH, looking over the ocean as the sun slowly sunk in the sky behind her. She was tired from the long plane ride and two-hour drive from Barcelona to the small coastal town that boasted its own castle and a pebbly beach perfect for sunbathing.

It was empty of sun-worshippers now, the small town's night life in full swing. It felt strange to be truly alone and she could not remember the last time she'd gone anywhere without her security detail.

She'd woken that morning in the bittersweet comfort of Sandor's warm embrace, her own hold on him just as strong. While her eyes were closed and his arms held her so securely, she could pretend he loved her. Once he'd woken, he'd made love to her and then…he'd left. After telling her that she had the weekend to think.

It was so typical of him to put a time limit on her ruminations, but the fact that he was giving her that time without further argument shocked her. It really did. It was so out of character for him.

Or was it? How well did she know him? She loved him, but that didn't mean she had an automatic in to the way his mind worked. Her dad would never have given an opponent time to regroup. Sandor hadn't even tried to tell her she had no reason to be scared. He'd said he expected her to come to terms with that truth on her own.

He'd stood there in front of her door, his big hands cupping her face and said, "You will either accept me for who and what I am, what I am capable of giving you, or you will not. You will either realize you have nothing to fear from me, or you will allow your fears to derail our future. It is your choice."

Then he'd kissed her and walked out the door.

While she doubted she would come to the conclusion that she had nothing to fear, she was rapidly approaching the one that life without him seemed much bleaker than life with him and without his love. Her own love was the biggest weapon against her in this battle. A battle that no matter how much the wounded parts of her heart left bleeding by her dad's lifelong indifference told her she had to win, she was uncertain of. Because the stronger, more complete part of her heart—the part that loved Sandor and believed in life's possibilities no matter what pain her past held, said the battle was in living and she was better off fighting for love than against it.

Sandor was everything she could imagine in a lover, but so much more, too. He was loving…to his mother. He was caring…with her. He was fair. He was honorable. And he was just so darn good. She couldn't believe the way learning he could never lie to his mother had impacted her.

His grandfather's strictures on integrity had taken deep root inside Sandor Christofides. And that just impressed Ellie to death.

Her dad had no problem lying to Ellie when he thought it was for her own good, but then he didn't love her. Not really. She'd wondered before if he'd ever loved anyone. Her mother? She got the feeling that losing her mom right after Ellie's birth had destroyed his heart. But she could be wrong. She had no way of knowing.

Both sets of her grandparents had died by the time she was six years old. Her dad's father had died of a heart attack at work the year Ellie turned six and his mother had been gone before Ellie had ever been born. Her mom's parents had died in a car accident caused by a drunk driver going the wrong way on the freeway two years before that.

She hadn't told Sandor the complete truth last night. She had been loved once. She could remember the warm feel of her grandmother's arms around her when she was really little. The way her grandpa had smiled at her as if she was the sunshine in his sky, but it had been so long, sometimes she forgot what it was like to be loved.

She remembered that warmth when she was around Hera, though. The older Greek woman made Ellie wonder what it would be like to have a mother. And part of her craved marriage to Sandor because she knew that if she married him, his mother would become her mother and someone in the world would actually love her. Sandor, who refused to acknowledge the emotion had no idea how very lucky he was to have had not one, but two people love him in his life.

And now she loved him, but she didn't know if she loved him enough to give the emotion freely without expectation of its return. If she couldn't, would their marriage work? Could it work? Was she strong enough to love unrequited and not grow bitter? And if she wasn't, how *real* was her love?

The answer to many of her questions lay in her response

to her dad. She looked inside herself and felt a measure of peace steal over her. Because while she got frustrated with her dad and sometimes the pain of not being loved like she needed hurt more than she wanted to admit, she'd never, ever hated him. She didn't hate him now. She never would.

And for all their similarities, Sandor was not a carbon copy of her dad. He paid her more attention than her dad ever had. He also showed tolerance for family priorities with his mom. That was something. Because Ellie wasn't going to raise her children alone, a work-widow. She got the feeling that Sandor would think it was doubly important for him to be there as a dad for his children. Because his own father had not been there for him.

She couldn't help wondering how he was going to react to learning she'd guaranteed herself more than a weekend to make her decision. She'd taken the week off from work, managed to fool her security detail into thinking she was still in her apartment and flown to Barcelona. She hadn't had any real destination in mind when she arrived at the airport; she'd simply taken the first international flight available.

That had landed her in Barcelona, where again she'd made her travel plans based on availability and hopped the first outbound bus with an empty seat. That had brought her to this small coastal town. She'd never ridden a bus before and it had been kind of neat.

She'd checked into an older hotel, the kind that still used high ceiling fans instead of air-conditioning to control the heat. Her room was small, but clean and the decor was old world with a charm often missing in the upscale hotels she stayed at when traveling under her father's aegis. She liked it, too.

Just as she enjoyed sitting on the beach for this short

moment in time as if she was just anyone, not the daughter of a super wealthy businessman. But it couldn't last. She had to go back to her life eventually.

When she left Boston, she'd been running, she freely admitted. From Sandor. From her own feelings. From the decision she fatalistically realized was a foregone conclusion. Especially since allowing Sandor into her body. He'd been right. She'd been arguing semantics. Once she'd given herself to him, there had been no hope.

Not for a future without him if he wanted to share hers.

Remembering back to just before they first made love, she'd had that moment of lucidity…the point at which she'd realized the outcome if she gave in. Stupidly…or courageously? Or simply unavoidably…she'd given in anyway.

She knew that sex didn't mean the same to women that it did to men. She didn't need her own painful past to learn that, the media screamed the message in every medium. But that sure knowledge had not saved her. Simply *because* sex meant something so different to her, she'd had no chance. If it was only her body she was holding back, she could have done it, but once her heart was involved, she was lost.

She was going to marry Sandor. The alternative…life without him and life without the mother's love she would be gifted with in Hera, was an untenable choice.

Her heart beat a rhythm of hope as she accepted the decision. Sandor wasn't her father. He loved his mother, which meant he was capable of the emotion. And he cared about Ellie. He was afraid of love as surely as she feared the emptiness of a life without it. She would teach him that love did not always hurt, that it could be the biggest blessing in a person's life. She'd seen it in the lives of others and she had known in that place all certain knowledge is born, not learned, that it would be the same for her if she had it.

He had reasons for his fear, just as she had reasons for hers, but that didn't mean he couldn't learn something new. She was taking a chance.

She refused to believe he had any less courage than she.

Ellie stayed in Spain for the rest of the week, missing Sandor, but reveling in the freedom. The security team didn't catch up with her until Thursday. After a very different return trip to Barcelona, this one in a chauffeured car, she flew home, this time first-class, Friday afternoon.

Sandor flipped open his cell while he clicked the send button on an e-mail to a subordinate in Taiwan. "Christofides here."

"Sandor, it's Hawk."

"Have you found her?"

"Yes."

Something in the other man's voice alerted him. "Where?"

"She's in Spain."

"She said she wanted time to think. Apparently she decided she needed distance, too."

"And other things."

"What is that supposed to mean?"

"Check your fax machine."

Sandor lithely jumped to his feet and crossed the room to where his personal fax whirred. Two sheets were in the printer tray. He picked up the top one, it had Hawk's company's logo and said, "For your review."

The sheet underneath was a newspaper clipping in one of the smaller European tabloids. It was obviously not a cover shot, but an interior article. It showed Ellie dressed much more provocatively and trendily than her usual attire. She was with an attractive dark-haired man standing beside a casino table. The man had his arm around Ellie's shoulder and his expression was nothing short of possessive.

For some strange reason, Sandor felt like he couldn't breathe.

"Go back to your computer. I sent additional photos in an encrypted file."

Sandor didn't know how the other man knew he'd gotten to the fax machine and had looked at the tabloid picture proclaiming a well-known playboy had a new plaything, who had been labeled as nothing more than his "woman of mystery."

Evidently Ellie's identity was unknown. Considering the fact that she did not court publicity, he was not surprised. And if the playboy was as wealthy as he looked, he could keep her name from even determined reporters.

Sandor checked his e-mail and there was the one from Hawk. He opened it, typed in the password Hawk fed him over the phone and a picture materialized on the screen. It was of Ellie and the man kissing on the beach. He scrolled down and the pictures got more condemning. Ending with one obviously taken through a window of the couple together in bed…naked.

"Destroy the pictures at your end," he barked.

"Done."

"Thank you, Hawk."

"I'm sorry, Sandor."

Sandor nodded and hung up the phone, realizing as he did so that Hawk would not have seen his head's movement.

The pain of betrayal tore through Sandor as he tried to

wrap his mind around the evidence presented to his eyes. Ellie had slept with another man.

He muttered a very ugly Greek word.

It did not help.

He'd believed she was a woman of integrity. He had believed her when she said she loved him. So, what had this been? A last fling before marriage? He could not accept that. He wanted nothing of marriage to a faithless woman.

The pain coalescing inside him was from disappointed hopes he told himself. It had nothing to do with a lacerated heart. His heart had stopped bleeding a long time ago.

George Wentworth called an hour later. "The security team have located her."

"In Spain?" Why he asked when he had the evidence of the pictures right in front of him, Sandor did not know.

"Yes. She's flying home today."

"Thank you."

"So, are we on target for the merger?"

"We will discuss it after I have spoken to Ellie." Why he felt compelled to tell her that the relationship was over before he told her father, he did not know.

She'd shown that their relationship meant nothing to her.

"Fine, fine. I'll talk to you Monday then."

Sandor allowed George to think all was well and hung up the phone. They would talk on Monday, but it would not be about the full merger that would be based on marriage between Ellie and Sandor.

Ellie called Sandor when she arrived at her apartment Friday night. It was late and she was tired, but at peace about her decision.

Silence greeted her at the other end of the line when he picked up. It was his cell, maybe the connection was bad. Though she'd noticed that his cell phone had problems much less frequently than hers. Sandor just seemed to control whatever was around him better than the average person.

"Sandor?" she asked, trying to see if the call was still connected.

"I am here."

"I'd like to see you."

"Tomorrow."

"Okay. Do you want to come by here?"

"I will."

"When?"

"I will be there after breakfast."

"Great." Maybe they could spend the day together. She'd missed him.

The line went dead and she realized the call must have dropped. She didn't bother calling him back. She was too sleepy and she would be seeing him in the morning.

The next day, Ellie was up early. She didn't know what time Sandor considered after breakfast, but she was ready at seven-thirty. He didn't arrive until nine.

When she opened the door to him, he did not kiss her, or even smile.

She wasn't so reticent. Begin as you mean to go on. And she meant for her relationship with him to be affectionate. Not that she had a lot of experience with that, but they could both learn. She leaned up and kissed his chin.

He didn't tilt toward her so she couldn't reach his lips, but she didn't let that bother her. "I missed you."

"Did you?"

She stepped back, biting her lip. "You're upset I was gone for a week."

"You could say that." She'd never seen him look so cold and remote.

If she wasn't sure she was mistaken, she would think his brown eyes were filled with disgust. But that would be much too strong a reaction for her little burst of independence.

"Are you angry I took longer than the weekend to make my decision?" she asked, trying to gauge his mood exactly as she turned and led him into her living room.

She sat down on the yellow sofa.

He took a chair as physically far from her as it was possible to get in the room. "So, you have made your decision?"

She tried a smile. "Yes and you might as well get used to the fact that I don't take orders well. It will make our life together less bumpy if you accept it. I'm also not fond of the cold shoulder treatment."

"So, you desire to marry me?"

"Yes."

"That is interesting. I must wonder why."

Her buoyant confidence that had carried her home began to falter. This conversation wasn't making any sense to her. "You haven't changed your mind just because I was gone for a week."

"No, I did not change my mind because you chose to take longer for your decision than I told you to."

"Good."

"However, other considerations have come to light." That was definitely disgust in his eyes.

"What do you mean?" What other considerations?

"You were no virgin when we made love the first time."

"I told you I wasn't."

"But what I did not appreciate was that lack indicated a deeper flaw in your character."

"You consider my status as a nonvirgin a lack?" she asked carefully.

He simply looked at her.

"Should I then consider your similar status the same way?"

"I, at least, understand the meaning of fidelity to one partner."

"And you're saying I don't?" she asked incredulously. No way were they having this conversation. "Because I had one lover before you, you've decided I couldn't be faithful? I don't believe this."

"No."

"What are you saying then?"

"That you have done a very good job of hiding your true character, both from your father and from myself as well as my investigator. At least at first. Clearly you are very clever at leading a double life. I should salute your ingenuity. It takes much to fool my investigator and your father's security team, but you have managed it."

"Sandor, I don't know what you are talking about. I haven't hidden anything from you." Well, she hadn't told him the details of her single past liaison, but that would hardly fall under the misnomer of hiding her true character.

"On the contrary, you did a very good job of deceiving me. Looking back, I can see the signs I was too blinded to take heed of before."

"What signs?"

"The condoms. If you were so innocent, why did you have condoms the first time we made love?"

"Because I assumed you'd want to make love eventually and I didn't want to risk pregnancy."

His lip curled. "That is a convenient excuse, but not a realistic one. Until last week, I made no moves to take our relationship to the bedroom."

"I know, but—"

He sliced his hand through the air, cutting her off. "I do not wish to sit here arguing with you."

"What do you want?" Inside, everything was freezing, but she didn't feel numb. It hurt, like being outside in below zero weather without her gloves. Cold so biting, it cut to the bone. That's what her insides felt like…painfully frozen.

"To say what needs saying and go."

"Then say it," she demanded from between lips that could barely move.

He looked hesitant for a second, but then the cold mask descended again and he said, "Your father wants an heir for his business. You refuse to be that heir, so he went looking. He found me."

More shards of ice pierced her heart and somehow she knew this wasn't done. "What?"

"He offered an impossible to resist dowry. Half of his company upon marriage to you and a will stating the other half would go to our children upon his death."

She shook her head, denying her father's culpability and Sandor's as well. To accept that they could treat her like a piece of barter hurt too much to deal with. She was nothing to either of them. She never had been.

"Yes. However, even half of your father's shipping business is not enough to entice me to marry a woman who would sleep with another man when the sheets had not even cooled from sleeping with me. A woman who was supposed to be considering my proposal of marriage."

As she forced the words to penetrate her mind, they

began to take horrible shape and two facts became clear. The first was that Sandor thought she'd had sex with another man while she'd been away from him. The second was that she would never have known about the business deal he had with her dad if Sandor had not become convinced of the first fact.

"You believe simply because I went out of country sans my security detail for a few days that it naturally follows I was having sex with someone else?" she asked, finding that as difficult to accept as the knowledge that she'd been played like a pawn between the two men in her life she loved.

She was used to indifference from her father, not this all out brutality toward her feelings. And from Sandor she had expected so much more. What a fool.

"I do not make such sweeping judgments on that flimsy a pretext."

"Are you saying someone told you I was cheating on you?"

"In a way."

"Explain," she demanded, the cold inside her growing until she felt like she was filled with ice that would shatter with the next blow.

He dropped a manila folder on the coffee table.

She picked it up, refusing to hesitate or fear what she would find inside. She pulled out several sheets of paper. The top one listed a prominent worldwide detective agency. It looked like a fax cover sheet. Underneath it was a copy of a sleazy tabloid article. A woman was standing at a roulette table with a man. The woman could have been Ellie's sister, she looked so much like her.

She was thinner, though, by at least ten pounds. Her eyebrows were waxed to a popular thinness, whereas Ellie left hers untouched because they were tapered naturally. The other woman dressed in the latest sexy fashions and held herself with the confidence of a cover model, or an actress.

Ellie always looked so stiff in photos like this. It was as if she had a sixth sense the press was zeroing in on her and would tense up just before any shot. She really disliked having her photo taken. The fax was black-and-white, so Ellie couldn't tell what color of eyes the woman had or if her companion's hair was black or brown.

She flipped to the next page and one of her questions was answered. The man's hair was brown. The full color sheet photo was of the same woman and man, this time kissing on the beach. The woman wore a bikini and hip sarong. She was so thin, her bottom rib was outlined. She didn't look sick like some Hollywood starlets, but she was definitely ultrathin.

As Ellie flipped through the pictures, she realized the woman's eyes were the same color as hers. She looked even more like Ellie than a sister would. Except for the weight thing and a few other cosmetic differences, the woman could have been Ellie's double.

The last picture was of the two people in bed together. She felt like a voyeur looking at it, but she could not tear her eyes away because it spoke so deeply to her. As Ellie recognized the same vulnerable look on the woman's face as she herself wore after making love to Sandor, she knew this woman *was* her sister. She did not know how it was possible. She tried to tell herself the doppelganger was just that…some stranger who shared enough genetic makeup from a distant past that they looked like twins though were probably not even considered really related.

But her instincts screamed it was more. She knew somewhere deep in her soul, somewhere so primitive she could not deny it…that this woman was her twin.

Her father had told her that her mother had died after giving birth to her. He'd never said anything about another baby being born. But it had to be. And her father had lied to her. How she and her twin had gotten separated, she didn't know. And she didn't care.

All she knew was that out there was a human being who would have loved her because sisters loved each other. A woman she would have loved and been there for, too.

She turned to Sandor. "Get out."

"That is all you have to say to me?"

"No."

He looked like he was almost hoping she could explain the pictures, but that had to be a trick of the lighting. He didn't care. He'd wanted to marry her in order to make his business bigger. Even his mom had gotten it right, while Ellie had lived in dumb ignorance. Enough was never enough for Sandor and his company would always come first. Just like her father.

"I think you are contemptible."

That seemed to rock him back on his proverbial heels. "What the hell did you just say to me?"

"You lied to me. You said you wanted me, but all you wanted was my dad's company."

"You think to use this to justify your behavior?"

"No. I don't have to justify my behavior and yours is ir-redeemable. Get out of my apartment, Sandor, and don't come back. Ever."

He didn't move. "Ellie…"

"Stop talking and leave." Too much was going through her mind. Too much pain. Too many surprises. Terror that all she had believed about life and herself was one big deception.

"At least tell me why you went to him. Was he an old lover…was it a last fling?"

"I don't owe you any explanations."

"You came home prepared to marry me."

"Yes, more the fool me."

"Ellie, make me understand."

She stared at him. The words felt like a plea from the heart, but he didn't have a heart. He only really cared about his company, about proving he was bigger and better than his father. He didn't care about her. His deal with her dad and the fact he had not told her about it proved that.

"You said you couldn't hide truth from your mother."

"It is not the same."

"Patently. You love her and I am nothing more than a pawn my father and you have played between you. I could hate you, Sandor. I really think I could hate you."

He laughed harshly. "One of the things I found so intriguing about you is how much we had in common. Even to this. I could hate you, too, Ellie."

"Go away, Sandor." Hot tears burned her eyes. She blinked furiously, determined not to let them fall while he was still in her apartment. "I don't want you here. Not ever again."

He stood, a flash of weary pain sparking in his eyes before it disappeared to be replaced by that glacial cool he'd worn upon entering her home. "And I do not want to be here. It seems we both made a mistake believing we could trust the other."

"Yes." Her voice cracked on the single word.

Sandor stopped on his path across the hardwood floor, but then he straightened his shoulders and kept going.

CHAPTER EIGHT

ELLIE WANTED TO scream out in pain.

She'd felt this way once before and promised herself she'd never let herself be used again. She'd failed and it hurt. It hurt so much, she didn't know if she could keep the pain inside like she had the last time. It was too big. Too deep.

But then her love for Sandor was so much more intense than what she'd felt at nineteen, the two feelings did not even compare. She felt like there was a steel band around her chest and it was contracting.

She couldn't deal with it. It was too much. But there was nothing there…no one to help her through the pain. Nothing to blunt its shattering intensity.

Then her gaze slid to the pictures spread out on her coffee table. The truth. She had to learn the truth.

She grabbed the fax cover sheet and stumbled to the phone. Blinking away tears, she read the number listed for the agency's landline. There were offices all over the world according to the stationery, but the one that had generated this fax was in New York. Her fingers were clumsy and she had to redial twice before she got the number right.

The sender, a person named Hawk, no last name given,

was not in the office. She left her name and both cell and home numbers with the answering service, requesting he call her immediately. She told the service it was an emergency.

In her mind, it was.

She couldn't let herself dwell on Sandor's betrayal. She heard you could not die from a broken heart, but you could not tell that by the way she felt. She couldn't afford to let the wound inside her grow. She had to contain it, lock it away with all the other pain of past rejection.

Desperation clawed through her as the agony threatened to shred her. She picked up the pictures and rushed to the computer, determined to research what she could. Anything to keep her brain occupied with something besides her bleeding heart.

She started with the article in the tabloid. Hawk had efficiently supplied the name of the weekly along with the page the article had been found on. She found the paper online. It was a Spanish tabloid, but since she was fluent in the language, that wasn't a problem for her.

Only there was no additional information. The name of the man with the woman who looked like Ellie's twin was given in the original article. Ellie did a site search on his name and discovered several more articles on him. But all that did was depress her.

Apparently she and her sister both had lousy taste in men because this guy had dated a half dozen women in the last year that he'd been photographed with. Who knew how many others he'd been with? There was no follow-up article to the one with his mystery woman.

Then Ellie decided it was time to go to the source. Her work with the unemployed had taught her how to research a person's background for the purpose of supplying sufficient documentation to get into continuing education programs. She started searching for her own birth records and from there, record of any sibling's birth.

She'd been at it about forty-five minutes when she stopped, so shocked, her eyes could barely focus enough to read the words on the computer screen. She *had* been born a twin and according to the records she was looking at, there was no record of her sister's death.

Following a hunch, she called a friend at the library. The other woman was a former client Ellie had helped to get into night school and eventually into a position as a reference librarian for a small town west of Boston. She asked the librarian to do a microfilm search on newspaper articles with her family's name in them around the time of her birth.

Two hours later, her friend called back with news that rocked Ellie's world right off its axis.

Ellie wasn't surprised to find her father in his office on a Saturday afternoon, but he was surprised to see her.

He stood up from his desk, a smile of welcome curving his lips. "Eleanor, what are you doing here?"

"I came to ask why you lied to me."

"Lied to you?" His pale blue eyes narrowed warily. "About what?"

"What's the matter? Are there so many lies between us that you can't guess which one I'm angry about?" she asked scathingly.

"I told Sandor not to mention the business deal. I knew it would only upset you."

"I don't care about the business deal between you two sharks."

"You don't?"

"No."

"So, you're going to marry him anyway?"

"Never!"

George Wentworth seemed to shrink, looking older than his fifty-four years. "I thought…"

"Whatever you thought, you were wrong. But I'm not here to discuss Sandor, or the almost disaster I narrowly avoided in marrying him."

"You aren't?"

"I'm here to discuss her." Ellie threw a picture on the desk.

It was one in which her sister's lover was difficult to recognize. Ellie had no doubt that her father would start looking for her sister, but the fact that he'd stopped looking at all and filed his lost daughter away with other bad business made her determined not to make it easy for him. She was perfectly capable of finding the other woman, or at least as capable of hiring a good detective agency as he was.

Her dad stared down at the picture and turned gray. "Where did this come from?"

"Ask Sandor."

His head snapped up. "What does Sandor have to do with it?"

"He thinks I cheated on him."

"But I told him you were in Spain."

"Did you?"

"Yes."

"There are stalking laws in this state. Call off your security detail, or I will invoke them."

"Damn it, Eleanor, you know I can't do that. It's not safe."

"You mean like she was safe?"

If anything, his complexion turned more pasty. "There was nothing I could do once she was gone. No leads to follow."

"You gave up."

"It was the only way to maintain my sanity." He made a visible effort to swallow. "How did you find out about her?"

"Certainly not from you."

He flinched, but said nothing.

"I played a hunch and had a newspaper search done of the time near my birth. The kidnapping made the papers."

"By the time it did, there was no hope left."

"Why didn't you tell me about her? I had a right to know."

"What would have been the use? By the time you were old enough to understand, I knew we would never see her again. Knowing about her would only have hurt you."

"Since when did you ever care whether or not I was hurt? You didn't tell me about my sister because you didn't want me to keep after you to find her. You knew I would. I'm stubborn that way about the people I love."

"I couldn't stand it. It hurt too much," the admission came out in a low, tortured voice.

"What hurt exactly? Writing your daughter off like bad business?"

"I didn't write her off. There was nothing to go on," he practically shouted, surging to his feet behind the desk.

"Who said I was talking about her?" Ellie asked, then turned and left his office.

He called her name, but she ignored the plea in his voice, just as he had ignored her pleas for affection for twenty-four years.

When she got home, there was a message on her answering machine. It was Hawk.

She called him back, irritated all over again by men whose priorities didn't match hers.

"I told your answering service it was an emergency," she said after he picked up and without even identifying herself.

"Miss Wentworth?"

"Yes."

"It has only been five hours since you called."

"An emergency implies immediate reaction is necessary, Mr. Hawk. I'm surprised your clients are tolerant of your definition."

"You are not one of my clients."

"Nevertheless…"

He sighed. "I will admit that I would prefer not to have this conversation, but to clarify, the demise of a relationship due to information I provide is not a five-alarm fire in my book."

"It should be when you got your facts wrong."

"Please, Miss Wentworth. I've heard it all before. Tearful begging and bribery are going to meet with the same non-results. Nothing is going to convince me to call my client and tell him there was a mistake. There was no mistake."

"You're so sure of that?"

"Absolutely positive."

She shook her head at his arrogance, but only said, "I have no interest in you calling the deceiving rat who employed you."

"Then what do you want?" the man asked, sounding skeptical.

"I want to know where you, or your operative was, when these pictures were taken."

"I cannot answer that question. My operatives are all very good at being discreet. Do not feel badly that you did not realize one was following you."

"I don't mean where the operative was in relation to the people in the pictures, I mean where he was geographically."

"He was in Spain," Hawk replied in a tone that said he was humoring her.

"Spain?" she choked out in disbelief.

The article had been in a Spanish tabloid, but the playboy with her sister was something of a Spanish celebrity, being a member of the family that ran one of the country's largest privately held business conglomerates. The article did not give any information regarding location of where the picture was taken with the man's mystery lady however.

"You know he was."

"No, Mr. Hawk. I don't know." She felt sick. She'd been in the same country, even on the same coast from the look of things, with her sister. "What city was he in?"

"Is this game necessary?"

"Just answer my questions and then I'll hang up and leave you in peace."

"The pictures were taken in and near Barcelona."

"If I'd stayed in the city, I might have seen her," she breathed incredulously. Why had she taken the bus out of the city to the smaller town further down the coast? Because she'd been running from Sandor. Pain sliced through her and she cut those thoughts off midspate. "Did you follow this couple anywhere else?"

"No. My client told me to stop surveillance so I called my operative in from the field."

At least she had a place to start. And a name. The playboy her sister had been seen with.

"Mr. Hawk, can you recommend an agency to help me find someone?"

"You're asking me for a recommendation?"

She almost laughed at his incredulity. "Yes. Sandor used you, which means you're the best there is. It follows you would know who I should call if I can't use you."

"Who do you want to find, Miss Wentworth, if you don't mind me asking?"

"The couple in the pictures you took. Specifically the woman."

"No agency I recommend is going to fabricate evidence of a second woman to get you off the hook."

"I'm not on the hook. In fact, because of you…I'm off of it permanently. Which gives me two things to thank you for, Mr. Hawk."

"Just Hawk," he growled. "What two things?"

"If you hadn't screwed up, Sandor never would have told me about the business deal he and my father intended to use me as the contract guarantee for. I might have married him. That's the first thing. And because you took those pictures, I now know I have a sister and even where to start looking for her. If you weren't in New York and I hadn't come to the conclusion that all men were a waste of good DNA, I might be tempted to kiss you."

Sandor stared down at the pictures of Ellie and the other man. When he'd first gotten the photos, he'd looked at them only long enough to assimilate what he was seeing and then he'd refused to look at them again. He'd meant to delete the images off his computer after he printed them off, but he hadn't.

Then he'd gone to Ellie's and told her it was over. And now he sat like a moonstruck calf, looking at the pictures in obsessive, meticulous detail. Ellie looked thinner in the pictures, but that wasn't right. Wasn't the camera supposed to add ten pounds? And there was something different about her eyebrows.

He tried to think back to when he'd met with her earlier. Had she looked any different? He couldn't remember. He'd been upset, damn it.

He didn't like admitting that any more than he liked the fact that he couldn't seem to look away from the pictures of his woman with another man. She *was* his woman. Ellie belonged to him. But if she'd gone to bed with another man, she wasn't his. According to the way they'd left things when he'd walked out of her apartment, she wasn't his. He'd even agreed to it.

His pride had. It had demanded he leave rather than push for explanations she was unwilling to give. Not that any explanation could make it okay. He was disgusted with himself for even wanting to know what she'd been thinking. For wanting to *understand*.

Only he couldn't get past one salient fact. She'd come home prepared to marry *him*. Why? Why, if she wanted to have sex with another man had she been willing to marry him? He knew it wasn't the money. It wasn't his position, either. Those things did not hold sway for Ellie. Or so he had believed.

But he had also believed her incapable of infidelity.

They were not married yet, but once she had taken him into her body, she had belonged to him. He crumpled one of the pictures in his hand as thoughts of her with another man tormented emotions he refused to acknowledge. He should not feel like this. If she wanted someone else, he should be able to deal with that the same way he did a business deal that fell through.

But he'd told her their relationship was not a business deal. And it wasn't. It was more, damn it.

He stared down at the picture again. Why did his instincts keep telling him something wasn't right about the photos? Obviously he didn't want to see his woman with another man. That was what was wrong.

He stared at the one of the woman on the beach. Was it a trick of the camera, or did Ellie's body look as different as he thought it did?

His phone rang and he picked it up. "Christofides."

"Sandor, it's Hawk."

"Yes?"

"I just had a strange phone call from your fiancée."

"We aren't engaged." Saying the words out loud made him feel hollow and he had to concentrate on ignoring the reaction.

"That's what she said."

"Was she angry with you?"

"No. Actually she thanked me."

"You find that strange?" Actually he did, too. He wouldn't have anticipated Ellie thanking Hawk for exposing her activities with the Spanish playboy.

"Not after she explained. She seems to think you and her father have messed her over royally."

Sandor made a noncommittal male sound he knew Hawk would understand.

"She asked for a recommendation for a firm to help her find someone."

"Who?"

"The woman in the picture."

Everything inside Sandor froze. "She's claiming it's not her?"

"Yes."

"And she wants you to find this other woman?"

"Not at first, no. She wanted me to recommend another agency. But if the woman in the photos is not your fiancée, then my operative made a mistake. That puts my agency at fault. I don't like mistakes, Sandor."

"I am aware of it. That is why I use your agency exclusively." He paused. "Are you going to find the woman?"

"Yes, but I wanted to give you the courtesy of knowing I was looking."

"I appreciate that."

"Sandor?"

"Yes?"

"I'm sorry."

Sandor knew the words were hard for the other man to say. He and Hawk shared that trait. They both hated making mistakes and admitting them equally as much. But the words meant something more. Hawk would not be apologizing if he wasn't convinced of Ellie's claim. If he believed her, then the evidence she had against the photos being her had to be pretty significant.

A sensation like heady relief washed over Sandor and he had to fight to keep his voice level. "Who does Ellie say the woman is?"

"Her twin sister, kidnapped from the hospital almost immediately after their birth. There were no leads and the baby just disappeared. No request for a ransom was ever made."

It took several seconds for Sandor to assimilate Hawk's words because they were so different than anything he would have expected the other man to answer. "I did not know Ellie had a sister."

"Neither did she."

"Her father did not tell her?"

"No and I get the feeling he's on her black list at the moment."

"Along with me."

"Afraid so."

Sandor swore, but he still felt lighter than he had in a long time. Ellie had not gone to another man's bed. She *was* his. "How did she find out?"

"She knew the pictures were not of her."

"So, she immediately thought she had a twin?"

"No. She told me she tried to believe the woman was just a doppelgänger, but her instincts were telling her otherwise, so she searched her birth records."

"And discovered another baby had been born?"

"Yes. I verified the birth records and newspaper accounts of the kidnapping as well as the fact that Miss Wentworth was staying in a small hotel in a town further along the coast than Barcelona during the time my agent was following her twin and Menendez around the city."

Trust Hawk to have double-checked the facts to be sure.

"I see. What are the chances they would have been in Spain at the same time?"

"Slim, but in my line of work, you learn to accept that kind of thing does happen. A lot more often than people want to believe."

"I believe."

"It upset her."

"You mean Ellie? What upset her?"

"That she was so close to her unknown sister and that they did not meet."

"She is no doubt upset about a lot of things right now."

Hawk's silence was agreement enough.

"Have you spoken to Wentworth yet?" Sandor asked.

"He's the next call I'm making."

"Let me know what you find out."

"No can do. Telling you I am looking is a courtesy, but in this case, Eleanor Wentworth is my client."

"Understood."

Sandor picked up the phone and dialed Ellie's number. She didn't answer and he wasn't surprised. She had caller ID. He tried three more times before deciding his best alternative would be to do what they had both said they did not want for him to do ever…return to her apartment.

He'd changed his mind, but he was under no illusions that she was in a similar place. Getting through the door was going to be no easy task. She'd said she never wanted to see him again. And she'd meant it. But he had not gotten to where he was by giving up.

He was on his way to her apartment when his cell phone rang.

It was Hawk again.

"What is it?" he asked without preamble.

"When I called to try to talk to George Wentworth, I discovered he had been rushed to a nearby private hospital. He was found collapsed on his office floor two hours ago."

"Did someone call Ellie?"

"She's not answering her phone."

"I am on my way to her apartment right now."

"Good. When you see her, tell her I'm working on finding her sister."

"Will do."

He tried calling Ellie's apartment again, but there was still no answer.

His next call was to his mother. That conversation was

almost as difficult as the one he anticipated with the woman he fully intended to claim once again.

Sandor knocked on Ellie's door, having gained access to the building without her assistance. She hadn't been answering her apartment buzzer, either.

There was no answer to his knock. That did not surprise him, either, but he did not give up, knocking again. No sound came from the other side of the steel door.

The next time he knocked, he called her name. Then called out, "Ellie, it is Sandor. I have news of your father."

Still nothing.

He strode quickly to the apartment that housed her security detail and banged on the door.

A tall man in his fifties, but obviously fit, opened the door almost immediately. "Yes?"

"You know who I am."

"Yes, sir."

"Has Miss Wentworth left her apartment this evening?"

"No, sir."

"Are you certain?"

"We have taken additional precautions since the slip she gave us last week, sir. There is no way she has left the building without us being aware."

Sandor nodded and turned, going back to Ellie's door and pounding on it until he heard a voice from the other side.

"For goodness' sake, Sandor, one of my neighbors is going to protest the disturbance." Her words were muffled by the door, but the scolding tone was clear. "Go away."

He stared straight at the peephole, hoping she was looking through it. "No."

"I'm not letting you in!"

"Your father is in trouble, Ellie."

"Yes, he is." She sounded both angry and hurt.

Sandor grimaced, hating having to impart this news. She had been through enough today, but there was no help for it. "He is in the hospital as we speak."

Silence reigned on the other side of the door. Then his cell phone rang.

It was her. He flipped it open. "I am sorry, *pethi mou*."

"What do you mean he's in the hospital?"

"Hawk informed me that he was discovered collapsed on the floor of his office over two hours ago. He was rushed to a private hospital."

The phone went dead. Then the bolts *snicked* signaling she was unlocking the door and then it opened. She stood with her hand on the knob, her eyes a chilly blue, the green almost completely absent. They were also red and puffy. "This had better not be a trick."

"I would not make something like this up."

"So you say."

Sandor did not take umbrage. He was well aware he could not afford to in their current circumstance. He was firmly in the wrong and they both knew it. What he did not know was how to undo the damage of their earlier conversation. He thought she could forgive him for believing her unfaithful; the evidence had been overwhelming. But he did not think she would forgive the business agreement he had with her father where she played a key role.

Sandor sighed. "As I said, George was discovered collapsed on his office floor this afternoon. His staff has been trying to reach you, but you are not answering your phone."

"I don't want to talk to him or you."

So, she had ignored caller identification that had indicated him, his company or her father's company. "I understand."

"No, you don't." Her chin trembled. "You don't love me. You can't understand at all."

CHAPTER NINE

HE DID NOT KNOW what to say to that. "I will take you to the hospital."

She shook her head, but he could see that her slim body trembled. "I can drive myself."

"You should not drive in your current state."

"What state is that, Sandor?" Anger leaked into her gaze. "Bleeding inside after finding out how thoroughly you and my father deceived me?"

"I knew nothing of your sister's existence."

"But you knew about the business merger. You knew that you saw me as nothing more than a contract guarantee. You were set to use me until you got what you considered evidence that proved me unworthy of being your pawn."

"That is not the way it was." But he'd known she would see it that way. Women and men did not think the same. He and Ellie seemed even further apart in the way they processed certain information than most. "I did not plan to use you. I wanted to share my life with you."

She shook her head. Denying his words? Denying herself? He did not know.

She swallowed convulsively, clenching her jaw to stop

her chin trembling. Yet he sensed the stoicism was only a step away from emotional breakdown. Something in the fragile way she held herself.

"I'm not going to discuss this right now." She sounded firm enough, but then she just seemed to crumble. "Is he really in the hospital?"

He pulled her into his arms rather than let her drop to the floor. "Yes, *pethi mou*. I called to check his condition on the way over here. He is stabilized, but they do not know yet what caused it."

He was grateful, but surprised when she did not pull away.

"*I* know," she mumbled against his shirtfront and then her lithe body shook with a sob. "It's my fault."

"No. That is not true."

"I told him about her. About my sister. Without any warning. Then I accused him of giving up on her and me. Then I left. I wouldn't listen to anything he said."

If he had realized the woman in the photos was not Ellie, he would have been with her when she confronted her dad. He could have made it better for both the woman he wanted to marry and her father. But he'd been deceived by his own eyes and now they would all pay the price.

"Shh…" He smoothed his hand down her back. "You were hurt. I should have been there with you. If we had not argued, I would have been. I am sorry."

She pulled away, somehow managing to stifle the emotions emanating off of her like an electric storm. She wiped at her eyes with the back of her hands and sniffed. "We need to go. I have to see him."

Sandor breathed a silent sigh of relief that she had decided to let him take her. She needed him even if she did not realize it.

They were in the car when Ellie asked, "How did you know about my sister?"

"Hawk called."

"Oh." She sighed. "That's right. You said something about talking to him. He told you about my dad?"

"Yes, in a later phone call."

"It was so shocking to find out I had a sister."

"No doubt horrifically so for you. But I had begun to suspect something was not right with the photos before I spoke to Hawk."

"What...why?"

"The woman in the pictures looks like you, but there are subtle differences."

"Why didn't you notice those before you accused me of sleeping around?" He could feel her intent stare as he negotiated city traffic.

"I was too angry to look at the pictures closely at first."

"But you weren't too upset after?" She sounded very confused.

"After you threw me out of your apartment, I went to my office. The pictures were there..." He let his voice trail off, unwilling to admit to the compulsion to be connected to her even if it was through looking at pictures of her with another man.

"And you looked at them?"

"Yes."

"Closely enough to notice the differences in the way my twin and I look?"

"Yes," he ground out.

"I would have thought you'd burn them and say good riddance."

"They were on my computer hard drive."

"Delete them then."

If doing so could have erased the feelings that came with looking at them, he would have. Nevertheless, he said, "I am glad I did not."

"Why?"

"I saw the truth."

"But I bet you didn't accept it until after Hawk's phone call."

"You are right."

"But you found it comforting?"

"Yes."

"I'm not sure I understand why. Since your watchdog was so obviously observing the wrong person, there's nothing to prove that I wasn't having a hot affair with some Spanish stud at the same time. Maybe I discovered the joys of fulfilling sex with you and decided to experiment a little."

He tried not to let her flippancy get to him. In some ways he definitely deserved her derision, but a primitive part of him wanted to growl at her to shut up. He did not like those words coming out of her mouth. "You came home prepared to marry me, you would not have done so if you were interested in experimenting sexually with others."

"Maybe I decided you were better in bed than my other experiments."

He couldn't help it. A growl escaped. "You would not do that," he said as evenly as he could, his grip on the steering wheel white-knuckled.

"That's not what you said this morning."

"I believed the evidence of my eyes." Maybe he had been premature in believing she would understand and forgive that aspect of their argument more easily than the other.

She turned to look out her side window, creating a mental distance that was intolerable. "It doesn't matter."

"I do not agree," he ground out. "I owe you an apology."

"For what?"

"For not trusting you. For accusing you of infidelity."

"We aren't married, I can't be unfaithful to you. Even if I had sex with ten other men—and you can't be sure that I didn't—it wouldn't mean I was unfaithful."

"You did not have sex with someone else. Stop implying you might have."

"Why?"

"You are goading my temper."

"So?"

"So, I do not want to have another argument with you."

"Maybe I do."

"Later…when you are not so fragile, pick a fight. For now, please…I am pleading with you, Ellie. Stop provoking me."

She gasped as if in shock.

Did she think he did not care enough about her to put his pride aside to protect her? He was not so weak.

After a couple of tension-filled minutes of silence, she sighed. "It really doesn't matter, but I didn't have sex with anyone else," she grudgingly admitted.

"I know."

"That doesn't make any difference. I'm not going to marry you, Sandor. You may have decided you can trust me, but I *know* I can't trust you now. That's not going to change."

He did not agree. "Because of the business merger?"

"Yes."

"We will overcome that."

"No, we won't."

They arrived at the hospital and he accepted now was

not the time for this conversation. He had lost ground with Ellie, but she had come home willing to marry him. He would bring her to that place again. "We will discuss this later."

"There's no point."

Instead of arguing, he parked the car and went around to help her out of her seat. Her face was pale, her eyes were still red and once again filled with moisture.

He leaned down and kissed her temple. "He will be all right, *pethi mou*. He is a tough man."

"I know." But, once again, she had to blink away tears.

He clasped her elbow and took it as a good sign that she did not pull away. It also disturbed him. George was not the only tough Wentworth. For Ellie to be willing to lean on Sandor feeling toward him the way that she did, she had to be feeling incredibly vulnerable.

He slid his arm around her waist and kept her close as they entered the private hospital.

Ellie walked into the hospital room, a cauldron of emotions swirling through her. She was still angry with her father, but she felt guilt, too. There was pain there as well, both at his and Sandor's betrayals. And fear. Horrible, mind-numbing fear. She didn't want her father to die. He was all she had, even if they weren't as close as she would like.

He was awake, his light blue eyes fixed on her as she approached the bed. He didn't smile. He didn't speak.

She stopped about three feet from the bed, not knowing what to do. Wishing he, or Sandor, would say something. Her throat was too clogged.

Then George Wentworth did something he hadn't since she was very little and then so infrequently, her memories of it often felt like dreams. He put his arms out. "Come here, sweetheart. Please."

And she ran to him.

He pulled her into his embrace and held her tight against his chest and she started to cry. "I'm s-sorry, D-daddy. I d-didn't mean f-for this to h-happen."

"I know, baby, I know." He rubbed her back, his hold warm and strong. "You didn't do anything wrong. I'm here because of my own mistakes, not yours."

She lifted her head, trying to hard to control her tears, but they just would not stop. "But I s-said…"

"The truth." He cupped her cheek. "Listen to me, Eleanor. I've made a lot of mistakes with you. I've made a lot of mistakes period, but I'll never regret the words you said this afternoon. They woke me up. You gave me hope for the first time in over twenty years that I would see my other little girl again. And as angry as you were, you made me realize that I had a daughter who needed me now, if I never find your sister."

"How could you not know I needed you?"

Agony darkened his eyes. "For more than two decades, I've practiced at ignoring your needs because I could not deal with feelings at all. Not yours. Not mine. I was a lousy father and I wish I could go back and change the past, but I can't. When your mother died, I shut myself off. It happened so fast, by the time your sister's disappearance came to light, I was already closed off from my babies. I didn't try hard enough to find her. I accepted without question…" His voice broke and it was a second before he could continue. "When the investigators told me there were no more leads to follow, I didn't argue. A year after her disappearance from the hospital, the police put her case on indefinite hold due to lack of new information. I closed the case with the investigative agency I'd hired as well."

Unbelievably he started to cry, turning his head away from her. "I have no excuse. When I look at your childhood, I feel as if I shut you out as completely as I did her. I failed you both on so many levels."

The monitor beside his bed began to beep and a nurse came rushing in, followed closely by a doctor. Ellie tried to get up and out of their way, but her dad wouldn't let her go.

"No. It's just my heart. It will get better. It's not used to feeling and it's having a hard time with the new experience." His attempt at a laugh ended in a pain-filled wheeze, but he wouldn't let her go.

"Please, Daddy, let them take care of you. Please. I don't want to lose you again."

"You won't leave?" His tone was pleading, his normally strong voice choked with tears she'd never, ever seen him shed before.

"I won't go further than the hall, I promise."

"I love you, Eleanor. Please believe me. I know I've done a lousy job of showing it, but I love you more than my own life."

She didn't know if she believed him. She wanted to. So much. And she felt badly, but twenty-four years of neglect didn't get wiped out with even heart-rending tears and confessions of affection. For all she knew, his illness was making him maudlin and he'd go back to his distant self once he was feeling better. She didn't say any of that, though.

She gave him a watery smile. "I love you, too. I always have."

He let her go and she moved back so the doctor could get to him. Then she stumbled toward the door and Sandor was there, his arm around her, guiding her out of the room and into the hall. Once outside the door, he pulled her into his chest, sheltering her from the noise coming from the room and the sense of desolation trying to wash over her.

Suddenly another pair of arms was there, hugging her. And a warm, comforting scent. "Is she all right, Sandor?"

"She is strong, Mama."

Ellie lifted her head. "Hera?"

"Yes, my child. I am here." The older woman's eyes were filled with compassion. "Come, let us go to the waiting room."

"I told him I wouldn't leave the hall."

"The room, it is right here, off the hallway. Not more than ten steps. You will know instantly if he has need of you. Sandor will make sure of it, but child you need to sit down."

Sandor agreed and between the two of them, he and his mother managed to convince Ellie to go to the waiting room and sit. They took a place on either side of her on the small sofa against one wall. There was no one else there and Ellie was glad. She never fell apart like this. She'd hate to have strangers witness her weakened state.

Sandor had his arm around her shoulder and she leaned against him, drawing on his strength.

Hera held Ellie's hand with one of hers and patted it with her other one. "You have had a difficult day, no?"

Ellie gave a shaky sigh. "Yes."

"Sandor told me all about it."

Ellie's head came up at that and she looked from mother to son. "All of it?"

Hera's dark eyes so like her son's, were filled with compassion. "Yes. All. My son, he was very stupid, but you must give him some credit. He did not know of your sister any more than you did."

"Did he tell you about the business merger?"

Hera's expression turned infinitely sad. "Yes. He and your father, they do not understand a woman's heart, do they?"

"No. I don't think they do."

"I am sitting right here," Sandor complained.

"And you are lucky to be so. Do not push it, my son."

Ellie choked out a laugh. "He's been watching out for me. He came to get me. I wasn't answering my phone."

"I know. He called me from his car on the way to your apartment."

"I might not have known." Tears threatened again. "What if Dad had died and I didn't know it?"

"Do not think this way. All will be well."

Ellie nodded, choking back tears.

The doctor came into the room. "Miss Wentworth?"

Ellie looked up at him. "Yes?"

"We've sedated your father. He needs rest right now."

"What happened?"

"You've heard the phrase, 'His heart couldn't take it'?"

"Yes."

"That's exactly what happened. It's actually very rare, but the shock of learning your sister was alive and apparently combined with some painful personal inner revelations, it was all simply too much for him. The good news is that tests show minimal damage to his heart and he should enjoy a full recovery, but he needs rest and relief from stress."

"He runs a multinational company...I think he lives on the stress."

"He'll have to learn to live on something else for a while."

Ellie looked up at Sandor. "How?" That's all she asked, but she knew he knew what she meant.

"I will work with his executive officers and keep the company running smoothly. Hawk will find your sister and all will be well. Believe me, *pethi mou*."

"I want to, but I'm scared."

"You have to have faith," Hera said, squeezing her hand. "Sandor will help you."

"But…"

"Despite his ignorant handling of his courtship with you, he is a smart and capable man. He will protect your father from further business stress until he is well again."

"That is good to hear," the doctor said. "You can go home, Miss Wentworth. Your father will not wake for several hours."

"I promised I wouldn't leave."

"So, you will stay." Hera patted her hand again. "And I will stay with you. Sandor, you must go home and rest. You have much to take care of tomorrow caring for two big companies."

Sandor tried arguing, but it did him no good. Hera Christofides was more than a match for her son when it came to being stubborn. Sandor arranged with the doctor for the two women to share a room near her father. Wealth brought with it certain privileges, especially in a private hospital.

Ellie slept fitfully and was beside her father's bed before breakfast the next morning.

His eyes opened and he searched the room with his gaze, stopping when he saw her on the far side of his bed away from the door. He smiled, his expression filled with gratitude. "You're here."

"Where else would I be?"

"I wouldn't have blamed you if you'd gone home and refused to come back to see me."

"Ellie would never do such a thing," Hera said from the doorway.

"Mrs. Christofides, I did not realize you were here."

"Ellie needs me right now."

Those words were so sweet to Ellie's ears. No one had ever "been there" for her like Hera was insisting on doing, or even Sandor had done the day before, or with his phone call just after 6:00 a.m. that morning. He'd somehow known she wasn't sleeping and had called to make sure she was okay.

He had offered to come to the hospital, but she'd known he had enough to keep him busy with his company and her father's so she'd told him not to come.

"Thank you for being such a good friend to my daughter."

Hera waved her hand dismissively. "It is my pleasure. She would be my daughter-by-marriage soon if you and my son had not messed up so spectacularly."

George winced. "Point taken."

"*Ne*…yes, I can see that it is."

Ellie reached out to take her dad's hand. "We don't have to think about that right now."

He squeezed her hand convulsively, as if he was afraid she'd pull away. "I would like to talk about it, though…if you don't mind."

Ellie chewed her lip nervously. "I don't want you upset again."

Hera pulled a chair near his bedside and sat down. "I've spoken with the nurse in charge. Breakfast will be delivered in twenty minutes."

It was such a mundane sentence, but it broke the tension starting to permeate the room.

Ellie's dad nodded. "Honey?"

"Promise you won't get overwrought again."

He smiled at her use of the old-fashioned term. "I promise."

"What do you want to say?"

He sighed and smoothed his blanket before he began to speak. The uncharacteristic hesitancy caught at Ellie's heart. "I approached Sandor with the merger idea after the way I saw he looked at you."

"What are you talking about?" Sandor had looked at her?

Her dad met her gaze, his own unflinching. She could tell he was determined to be fully honest. "I won't pretend it was all altruism on my part. I'd realized long ago you had no interest in running the company. Taking on a partner who could give me grandchildren to inherit the company made sense."

"He could hardly make those grandchildren without my cooperation."

"Exactly."

"So you offered him half your company if he would marry me?"

"Yes, but Ellie, I knew he wanted you, too. Personally."

That was something she was still very much uncertain of, but she didn't deny her dad's take on it. She saw no point in doing so. Apparently he had believed Sandor wanted her and that's really all the was relevant to this conversation.

The thing was, he'd overlooked something pretty major in her estimation. "Is that supposed to make it all better? What about what *I* wanted?"

"You looked at Sandor Christofides the way your mother looked at me when we first met."

"Like what?" Ellie asked, more because she was hungry to hear about her parents and what it had been like between them than because she wanted to know how her dad thought she saw Sandor.

"Your mother looked at me like a hungry hunter. She was an adventurous woman, your mother. So, her sweet eyes, the same color as yours, they were filled with both wariness and attraction. She wanted to tame the lion, but wasn't sure I could be tamed."

"You were a playboy?"

"No. Like Sandor, I was a businessman. A shark. I'd inherited wealth, unlike your young man, but it wasn't enough for me. I was only twenty-eight, when I met your mother, but though we worked side by side for years, I'd already almost doubled my father's business holdings."

"Did you love her?"

"Very much."

Something inside Ellie cracked at that assurance. He had loved once.

"How did she die?" She'd always known her mother died after giving birth, but there'd been an accident, too. She'd never asked for details because, well…that wasn't the kind of thing she asked her dad and there'd been no one else.

"She was in a car accident. It was bad. She went into premature labor…she delivered you girls and then slipped into a coma. She never came out and died less than a week after giving birth."

"I'm sorry."

"I am, too. She was a wonderful woman and she would have been so good for you. I didn't raise you the way she would have wanted me to. I failed her and you both…just like I failed your sister. I fight for every business concession I want, but I was too weak to fight past the pain of her loss."

"Failure is not a terminal disease unless you allow it to

be," Hera said from her chair beside the bed, sounding comfortingly practical.

George's head snapped up and he met her gaze. "I'm not going to let myself die. I'm going to make it up to my girls. Somehow. Someway."

Hera nodded. "That is an admirable sentiment, but it will not be easy."

"I know."

"If it becomes too difficult and you retreat to your work again, you will not get another chance. Your daughter is very self-sufficient."

"Too independent."

"You would rather she was weak?"

"No."

"Good."

Ellie didn't mind the conversation that did not require her participation. She had a lot to assimilate and as much as she wanted to trust her dad again, she just didn't know if she could. He'd hurt her so many times both as a child and then as a woman. And she'd been hurt by others, too…she was discovering that past pain could be a huge barrier to present acceptance of things like love and affection.

CHAPTER TEN

BREAKFAST ARRIVED AND they ate together, setting the pattern for days to come. Ellie came to the hospital each morning and ate breakfast with her father before going on to work. She knew that Hera spent a couple of hours every afternoon with him and Ellie returned in the evenings to spend time with him before bed. Sandor spoke to him daily.

Sandor called Ellie two or three times a day, too, but they didn't see each other. He was working twenty hour days covering for her dad and taking care of his own business.

In a way, Ellie was grateful for the respite from his company. She knew that since he'd decided she was trustworthy, he still wanted to marry her. She just was not up to arguing with him about it right now.

Hawk was still looking for her sister, but the man she'd been seen with had disappeared from sight and Hawk's agents were having difficulty locating the tycoon. The investigator had learned what the tabloid reporters had…no one else seemed to know who Menendez's mystery woman was.

In the meantime, Ellie was getting to know her dad like she never had. He told her things about her mom, her grandparents…*himself* that she'd never known. And each day, she got a little closer to believing the change in him was a permanent one. That maybe he really did love her.

But part of her acknowledged that until he was back to work and in his old world and *still* interested in her life and spending time with her, she wasn't going to trust that change completely.

He went home from the hospital the following Friday afternoon. It was the longest break from work Ellie had ever known him to take. Even though the following day was Saturday, he went into the office for a few hours. Sandor made sure those hours were short, escorting him back home before lunchtime.

He'd arranged with Ellie to be there to share the meal with her father. She waited for them, butterflies playing volleyball in her stomach. She hadn't seen Sandor since the Saturday before.

When she did see him, she had to fight the urge to take him into her arms. He looked exhausted, but then running two multinational companies would be enough to drive most men into the ground. Not Sandor. He looked tired yes, but still so strong and masculine that Ellie's knees had weakened at the sight of him ushering her father into the room.

She'd set up fruit juice spritzers on a tray before their arrival and served both men as soon as they seated themselves.

Her dad had taken an armchair kitty-corner to where she sat. He reached for the drink. "Thank you, sweetheart."

"You're welcome. How did it go at work?"

"Sandor did an excellent job keeping everything running smooth. There wasn't much for me to do."

"There was enough to keep you there four hours," she said with a wry smile as she offered Sandor his drink.

He'd folded his six-foot-four-inch frame onto the

cushion beside her. He took the drink and winked. "He had to check everything I had done to make sure I had not messed anything up too badly."

"Baloney. I knew you'd handled everything fine, Sandor, but there are always things that simply cannot be delegated. No matter how savvy the delegate."

Ellie sat back down, keeping as much distance as she could between her and Sandor. "How are you feeling," she couldn't help asking him.

"Surely that is a question for your father."

"Dad looks healthier than I've seen him in a long time, you on the other hand are almost gray with fatigue."

"It has been a long week, but I survived it."

"You need more rest, Sandor."

He merely shrugged.

She frowned. "You aren't going back to the office after lunch, are you?"

"There are things I could take care of."

"Let them wait."

His dark eyes widened.

Her dad laughed. "She's getting bossy. That's got to be a good sign. With her mother it indicated she felt possessive of me."

Heat climbed into Ellie's cheeks. "Even if we are no longer dating, I still consider Sandor a friend. I don't feel possessive of him, but I care about him. As a friend."

It was a huge understatement, not to mention a lie. She did feel possessive toward him, but to admit it would imply he had rights over her and that she would not do. She loved him and one thing she'd realized over the last week was that love, no matter how battered took a lot to die. Hers was bruised and maybe even bleeding, but still very much alive inside her.

For both of the men now looking at her so speculatively.

"I would be happy to stay out of my office if you would agree to spend the afternoon and evening with me," Sandor said.

"I have things to do this afternoon."

"Like what?" her dad asked.

"I'm expecting a call from Hawk on the search for my sister. And I need to do some laundry and clean my apartment. I haven't been home much lately."

"I would be happy to help you do your laundry."

That made her laugh out loud. "I can just see that."

Sandor shrugged. "My mother and I had very little disposable income when we arrived in America. I can sort and fold clothing with professional efficiency, I assure you."

The thought of having him in her small apartment with her for several hours was nothing short of terrifying. "I don't think that's a good idea."

Sandor laid his hand on her thigh. "We need to talk, Ellie."

"I don't want to talk," she admitted in a low voice, wishing her dad was not there with them, overhearing their conversation.

"Please, Ellie…"

She closed her eyes against the appeal in his but nothing could stop the warm, rich tone repeating in her head. "I don't want to be hurt anymore, Sandor. Please don't push me."

She hated saying the words in front of her dad, but both men knew they'd hurt her. She wondered if they realized how much. She was working toward a relationship with her dad again, but she didn't know if she could ever give Sandor another chance. Not after learning she was nothing more than a business pawn for him.

Sandor sighed. "I won't push you *now, pethi mou*."

He wondered if she noticed the emphasis he put on the word, now. He knew she couldn't be aware of how damned fragile she looked. She needed rest as much as she claimed he did. So, he would not push her today, but soon, he and his Ellie were going to talk out their relationship. And she was going to give him another chance. She was too damned gentle and kind not to.

Besides, she'd said she loved him. He knew she'd meant it. If she was capable of turning off her emotions, she would have stopped loving her father a long time ago. She never had and it gave Sandor hope.

Hawk called the next morning with the news that he'd found Ellie's sister. She went by the name Amber Taylor and she was staying on Miguel Menendez's yacht with him. They'd just come into port after spending more than a week at sea.

Once Hawk knew her sister's name, he'd learned quite a bit more about her. She was a model, successful, but not with supermodel status. Which was why Ellie had never seen her on the cover of any major magazines. Amber did mostly fashion shoots and trunk shows with a few commercials. Ellie's lack of public profile had contributed to the fact that no one had ever latched onto her resemblance to a fairly successful model.

In addition, Amber had grown up in a small town in Southern California with her mother, Helen Taylor. Father deceased. Or supposed father. She'd only recently moved into international modeling circles and at twenty-four, her career was only a few years from peaking.

She didn't date much and her current relationship with Miguel Menendez was the first evidence Hawk could find

of her living with a lover. There was no evidence of a
formal adoption, but that had been expected. What had not
been expected was that she was living under the identity
of the baby daughter Helen Taylor had given birth to.

A baby who had been born premature and died soon
after birth despite the best efforts of the doctors at the time.

"I don't want the authorities brought in on this right
now, Hawk."

"I didn't think you would, Miss Wentworth."

"You aren't going to tell my father you've found her, are
you?" She wasn't sure how she wanted to deal with the information, but she didn't want to risk another shock that
could lead to a heart attack.

"You are my client, Miss Wentworth. Not your father."

"Right. Okay. Give me the information you have on her
current location."

She scribbled down what Hawk told her. Then she hung
up the phone. Considering how she was living, Ellie
doubted very sincerely that Amber knew anything about
her real family or that she even had another family.

Hawk was investigating the circumstances of her kidnapping further and trying to figure out how Amber had
ended up with Helen Taylor, who did not fit the profile of
a kidnapper in any shape or form. From all accounts, she
was a dedicated mother who had sacrificed a great deal for
her daughter to succeed in her chosen profession.

Not really sure why she did so, Ellie picked up the
phone to call Sandor after hanging up with Hawk.

He picked up on the first ring. "Ellie?"

"I just got off the phone with Hawk."

"Has he found your sister?"

"Yes."

"Where?"

"In Spain. She's been at sea on her lover's yacht, but they put to shore yesterday."

He said nothing.

"I don't know what to do, Sandor. Do I just show up out of the blue with no warning? Do I call her first and tell her I want to meet her? Her mom might very well be her kidnapper. How is she going to feel about that?"

"Tell me everything Hawk said."

Ellie did, leaving nothing out.

"Her mother does not sound like a criminal. In fact, she sounds very much like a woman who cares deeply for her daughter."

"I thought so, too."

"There must be extenuating circumstances."

"I don't want to hurt Amber."

"But the circumstances of her birth cannot be ignored."

"I know."

"Perhaps it would be best to wait until Hawk has discovered more about how Amber entered Helen Taylor's life."

And that's what she did, but as each day went by Ellie's stress levels increased. She missed Sandor, though he called her several times a day. At night, she craved the comfort of his arms around her. And no matter how many times she reminded herself that comfort was a false one, the feeling would not go away. She did not realize how much an integral part of her life he had become until he was gone.

She was the one the pushed him away. He invited her to dinner, to lunches, to the theater, and she turned down every invitation. He never got angry with her. Just reminded her that when the time was right, he was going to corner her and there was nothing she would be able to do to get out of it. The most frightening realization of all was that she wasn't sure she wanted to. In fact, a big part of her wanted him to take the choice out of her hands and simply show up at her apartment.

But he didn't and she didn't sleep, spending both the dark hours of night and the spare moments of her days worrying.

She wanted to tell her dad that Amber had been found, but was afraid of what it would do to him to hear the news.

Hawk called and said he couldn't find any indication of how Amber had come to live with Helen Taylor as her daughter.

"If she's not the kidnapper, Miss Wentworth, then I have no idea how she came to be your sister's mother."

Hawk had learned more about Helen and Amber Taylor during his investigation and it all pointed to Helen being as good a mother as Hera. It hurt to think it had all started with a kidnapping. She couldn't imagine how her sister would feel to find that out. Choking out a goodbye to Hawk, Ellie was already mentally dialing Sandor's number when she disconnected her call with the world renowned investigator.

Sandor swore in Greek when Ellie told him what she had learned. "I'm so sorry, *agape mou*. But we will not let this situation tear lives apart."

He said it with such confidence that she believed him.

"What am I going to do?"

"We begin by telling your father."

"We?"

"Naturally. You do not think I would leave you to do this thing alone, do you?"

She had no right to call on his support since their breakup, but she wasn't about to turn him down. "Thank you."

* * *

Sitting in his favorite armchair close to Ellie's place on the couch in his oversize living room, her father paled as Ellie told him all that Hawk had learned so far.

"So, this woman…Helen Taylor…most likely kidnapped my daughter and brought her up to believe she was the baby she had lost two months before?"

"Yes, that's what we think." Sandor held Ellie close to him with one strong arm and she wasn't about to protest.

Nor did she protest him answering for her. She was shaking inside from the stress and worried that talking about her sister was once again going to prove too much for her dad.

Ellie added, "Her husband had died in the tragic car accident that sent her into early labor. Hawk thinks the similar circumstance surrounding mine and Amber's births may have triggered the kidnapping."

"But the woman was a good mother?" her dad asked in a hoarse voice.

"From all that Hawk could discover, she was exemplary in every way. She really loves her daughter. She lives for her." Ellie kept the wistfulness from her voice.

It was wrong to envy her sister a lifetime with a loving parent, especially knowing that she would face the pain of difficult revelations soon enough. But part of Ellie couldn't help wondering what it would have been like to be raised by someone who considered her more than an adjunct in his life.

"I think we should approach Helen Taylor first," Sandor said.

"I agree." Her dad ran his hand over his face and sighed. "She's no doubt been living in abject terror of being caught out for more than two decades. We need to deal with her first."

Ellie had reached the same conclusion. "It's going to be

awful for everyone. I've never met the woman, but I can't help but pity her. Whatever led to her taking Amber, she really seems like a decent person who loves her daughter." She took a deep breath and said what needed saying. "I don't want the authorities brought in. This is going to be hard enough on everyone without that."

Her dad nodded. "We will find out what happened… why she took my daughter and kept her…and we'll go from there."

Relief that he was taking the news so well and that her father was being so tolerant flowed through Ellie. "You're a lot more understanding about this than I expected you to be."

He grimaced, his light blue eyes shadowed with guilt and pain. "I can't get past the fact that she gave Amber the love I withheld from you. Maybe you would have been better off if she'd taken you both."

Ellie didn't know what to say. She was a poor liar, so she could not claim she'd hadn't had the same thought. Until her dad had "gotten human" she would have questioned whether losing her would have impacted his emotions at all. She felt guilty for thinking that way and knew it was wrong, but she'd spent most of her life believing that if she were to disappear—for whatever reason— the only thing her father would feel is a sense of failure in living up to his responsibilities.

She was beginning to believe she meant more than that to him now, but twenty-four years of thinking a certain way did not disappear overnight.

Letting her heart lead, she dropped to her knees beside his chair and hugged him. "I don't regret the fact that you raised me."

That, at least, wasn't a lie. No matter what strange

thought had flitted through her head upon discovering each new aspect of this situation, she loved her dad. She always had. The more he told her about her mom, the more Ellie realized in that way, she took after the woman who had died before she'd had a chance to hold her babies.

His laugh was hollow, but his return embrace was tight. "You're a gentle soul, Eleanor Wentworth. Very much like your mother," he said, echoing her thoughts. "I didn't deserve her and I don't deserve you."

"Maybe," she allowed with a small smile as she returned to her seat beside Sandor, leaning against him slightly and drawing on his strength. "But you're stuck with me regardless."

"We'll fly to California to see Helen Taylor tomorrow," her dad decided.

Sandor's arm returned to her shoulder and squeezed. "I am going with you."

Ellie didn't even consider arguing. She craved his support. She turned to meet his dark gaze. "I would appreciate that."

He kissed her, his lips tender, his expression unfathomable. "Then it is settled."

They flew in Sandor's private jet to a small airport near the town that Helen Taylor called home. She wasn't sure why they'd taken Sandor's plane instead of her father's. But when Ellie asked, her father said only that Sandor preferred to do so. He and her dad worked while Ellie fretted, but hid it behind a facade of relaxed boredom while flipping through one of the fashion magazines that featured shots of her sister.

Hawk had provided a wealth of information on Amber's

career. Ellie had spent countless sleeping hours looking at pictures of her sister in "model mode" and wondering what went on behind her beautiful aqua gaze. Funny how the same color of eyes on Ellie felt like nothing special, but on her model sister, they looked exotic and mysterious.

She rubbed at her own eyes, wishing she could take a nap, but knowing sleep would be ever elusive. She simply could not turn her brain off. She'd done a good job of keeping up the stoic front she'd spent a lifetime cultivating, but underneath, she wanted to crumple.

But a Wentworth did not crumple and even if they did, she couldn't. Her father and her sister needed her right now.

They were less than an hour into the flight and Ellie was yawning for the fifth time when, without the slightest warning, she felt herself bodily lifted from her seat.

Gasping, she clutched at Sandor, the magazine fluttering to the floor of the cabin. "What are you doing?"

"You need rest." She wasn't having any trouble reading his expression now. He looked angry. "Have you slept a full night since the day you returned from Spain?"

"No," she admitted and let her head drop to lie in the curve of his neck. "But I'm not going to sleep now, either."

"We shall see."

She found herself smiling against his chest at his arrogance. "I can't. Honestly, Sandor. Too many things are whirling inside my head."

He ignored her words and carried her to the tiny bedroom in the back of the plane, kicking the door shut behind him once they were inside.

"This is pretty nice. My father's jet doesn't have a bedroom," Ellie remarked.

"I know. That is why we took mine."

"For the bedroom?"

"Yes. You are not sleeping. That is obvious to anyone with eyes. I was determined you would rest comfortably during the flight."

Unused to being cosseted, Ellie found herself swallowing a suspicious lump in her throat. Even if she couldn't sleep, she appreciated the gesture. A lot.

"Thank you," she whispered.

"You are welcome." He laid her down on the bed, arranging her so that her head rested on a nice fluffy pillow. "Comfortable?"

"Mmm…hmmm."

"Good." He sat on the end of the bed and took her shoes and thin socks off.

She wiggled her toes. "Um…thanks."

"Again…you are welcome."

But he did not stop there. Before she knew what he was doing, he'd unbuttoned her dark silk slacks and had them halfway down her hips.

She grabbed his wrists. "What are you doing? You can't undress me," she hissed in a fierce whisper, not wanting her father to hear.

Though it was highly unlikely, even in the well insulated cabin, flying created a lot of white noise that masked conversations even between people seated near one another.

"You cannot sleep with your clothes on. Relax, *pethi mou.* I will take care of you."

"I'm not going to sleep anyway," she protested. "There's no reason for me to get undressed."

"You will be more comfortable." With a deft move of his hands, he broke her hold on his wrists and had her slacks down her legs and off before she could do more than gasp. He folded them on a neat crease and hung them in the miniscule closet before turning back to face her. "Is that not better?"

Ellie could only gape. Whether it was from sheer shock or that combined with her exhaustion, but her mind wasn't working properly. She should have scrambled under the covers, but she lay there in her blouse and panties and wondered what he would do next.

She found out when he sat beside her and began to unbutton her blouse.

Finally getting some semblance of wits about her, she twisted away and jumped off the bed. "I think I'll leave my blouse on. In fact, I should probably put my slacks back on and rejoin Dad."

The look in his eyes said she was going to get undressed and in that bed, like it or not. Too bad he was on the side by the closet and coincidentally, the door through which she wanted to escape. Though not half-dressed as she was.

She crossed her arms over her chest. "I don't like being bossed around, Sandor."

He leaned back against the door, crossing his arms as well and giving her a look she was fairly certain outdid hers in the intimidation stakes. "I do not like seeing my woman ready to collapse from exhaustion."

"I'm not your woman."

He crossed that small room with the speed of a Jaguar and then stood towering over her. "We are at odds. I accept this. But you *are* mine."

"No," she whispered the denial that felt like a lie.

"Just as I am yours."

The words touched her deep inside where she did not want

him to go again. And she shook her head, unable to give voice again to the denial her heart said she should not make.

His hands curved around her shoulders and he stepped closer so their bodies were mere inches apart. "So, you do not care if I bed another woman?"

Her heart screamed a denial, but she merely said, "Don't be crude," in her best approximation at a distant tone.

"Do not lie to me," he countered, his tone pure male censure.

She swallowed, wishing he wasn't so close…or that his nearness did not impact her so much. "I have no right to stop you from going to bed with another woman."

"I give you the right."

She opened her mouth, but she could not force a rejection to his offer from her throat.

He kissed her, briefly but firmly. "I give you the right," he repeated.

She couldn't say a word. To refuse the right was beyond her, but to accept it carried far too many connotations she was not prepared to deal with. She tilted her head back and kissed him, just as briefly and much more softly.

His eyes closed and he inhaled a deep breath before opening them again. "We will get there," he promised her. "Now, come. Let me care for you."

He lifted her again and put her back on the bed, his movements careful as if he did not want to startle her, but the implacable expression in his eyes said he expected her to rest.

Then, his eyes filling with a tenderness she could not fight, he finished unbuttoning her top and pulled it from her body. He hung it up and while he was beside the closet, he hung up his jacket, too. Their gazes locked. She sat up and curled her arms around her knees, but did not protest

when he started taking off the rest of his clothes. He did
not break the eye contact while he stripped to his silk
shorts, neatly hanging everything up in the closet to be
donned again later.

He came back to the bed.

She licked her lips. "Sandor?"

"I, too, could use a nap, Ellie. I have slept poorly since
the night you disappeared from Boston. We will rest
together. And for now, that is all we will do."

She should argue, but deep inside, she didn't want to.
She trusted him not to push for anything sexual if he said
he wouldn't. And she wanted to be held. So much. Her
world was a maelstrom of frightening events and even
though he had betrayed her trust, Sandor looked like an
island of comfort for her storm-tossed heart.

Silently she uncurled from her protective position and
climbed under the covers, leaving room for him to lie beside
her. She wasn't sure, but she thought he sighed with relief.
He joined her, pressed the button above the bed to cut the
lights in the tiny cabin and then pulled her into his arms.

She didn't fight, but she didn't relax, either. She
couldn't. With loving came wanting and since her love for
him continued to beat inside her heart, her desire for him
was there, too. But she didn't want to act on it. She didn't
think she could handle it right now if she did.

She was barely holding it together and the way he made
her feel when he touched her would rip away the barriers
she'd manage to erect to protect herself since discovering
both his and her father's duplicity. Besides, he was
right…she both needed and wanted the healing rest of
sleep. She was hungry to be held and to feel safe, if for just
a little while.

He seemed to understand and did not try to cajole her into relaxing. He curled his big, warm body around her stiff one, wrapping his arms around her and spoke soft, soothing things into her ear until she grew drowsy. Bit by bit, her body gentled into his until she fell into a more restful sleep than she'd had since the last time he shared her bed.

She awoke sometime later to the sensation of someone gently brushing her cheek. Her senses told her it was Sandor before mind even became fully aware.

CHAPTER ELEVEN

"WAKE UP, *agape mou.* We will be there soon."

Her eyes fluttered open to a vision of him dressed and sitting beside her on the bed.

"I slept the whole flight?" she asked disbelievingly.

"You needed your rest."

She'd needed her rest the night before, too, but she'd tossed and turned until giving up on sleep and had gotten up before dawn to work on client files. "So you said."

"I was right."

"You don't have to sound so happy about it."

"What man does not like to be right?"

She wrinkled her nose. "I don't know one." It was all she could do not to snuggle into his hand. "I can't believe I slept so well."

"It was being held in my arms. I confess I, too, slept better than I have in weeks."

She scooted into a sitting position, holding the sheet against her chest. "Yes, well…we'll have to get matching teddy bears or something."

"Or something."

She wasn't touching that. "How long until we land?"

"Thirty minutes."

"Oh." She looked around the well lit, utilitarian cabin. Thank goodness there was a door to the small bathroom from the sleeping area. "I need to freshen up."

"You look very good to me, but I can understand you might think the just-been-loved look is better saved for our times of privacy together."

"I haven't been loved."

"Are you sure about that?"

What was he saying? That he loved her? No. He didn't believe in the emotion, but could he have changed his mind? Her dad had changed and she thought that was impossible. Had Sandor had some kind of emotional breakthrough? But if he had, surely he would have said something. Not made some oblique reference and expect her to get it.

She swallowed questions she wasn't sure she wanted answers to in her current emotional state and stared at him. "I mean we didn't have sex."

"That I concede. It comes later, I think."

"No," she breathed, more for form than vehemence.

He leaned forward until his mouth was a bare centimeter from hers. "Are you sure that is the word you will be saying?"

She opened her mouth to answer, but whatever she would have said remained locked in her throat because he kissed her. His mouth totally claimed hers, his lips molding to hers and his tongue sweeping her interior. Any protest she would have made died before she even breathed it and she kissed him back until she was panting and his hands were clenched in fists on either side of her hips.

"We will revisit this discussion later," he said and then stood up just as if he hadn't kissed her to within an inch of her life and made implications that were soul-shattering.

He tapped the end of her nose. "Get ready, Ellie *mou*. I will see how your father is holding up." Then he was gone.

Dazed, she climbed out of the bed and made a quick trip to the bathroom to brush her hair and other things before getting dressed again. Sandor had been right. She'd slept much better without her clothes and they were certainly fresher looking than they would have been if she'd worn them to bed.

The drive from the small municipal airport to Helen Taylor's home was less than an hour, but the tension inside the limousine was palpable by the time it pulled up in front of her modest ranch style home.

Ellie put her hand on her father's arm. "Are you going to be all right?"

His smile was reassuringly warm, so different than the way he used to look at her. "Yes, but what about you?"

"I'm scared," she admitted, surprising herself.

But then, maybe she was changing, too. Knowing you were loved changed the way you reacted to another person, she found.

He laid his hand over hers. "It is all going to be fine. Trust me, sweetheart."

"I don't want Amber hurt." Or her dad. Or herself. Or Helen Taylor, for that matter. Yet, she didn't see how at least some emotional bloodshed could be avoided.

"Neither do I. We're going to handle this the best we can and trust for the outcome."

She swallowed and nodded. He left the limousine first, then Sandor, who turned to help her out. He pulled her into his side with an arm around her waist as they walked up to the front door and she was grateful for the contact. Despite the warmth of Southern California's weather, she felt chilled. She cuddled against him in a public display of affection that she would not have shown a month ago.

Something inside her had definitely shifted.

Her father rang the bell. Less than a minute passed before it swung inward. A woman stood there, her wavy blond chin-length hair, cut in a bob and petite frame with trim figure proclaimed her Helen Taylor. She looked exactly like the photos taken of her recently as well as those Hawk had procured from years past. There was an almost fey quality about her that enhanced Ellie's already signaled protective instincts.

Helen's hazel eyes widened and darkened with distress as she seemed to recognize George Wentworth. Her gaze skimmed to Ellie, jolted up to Sandor's impassive features and back to Ellie again. "You look just like her. You look just like my baby."

Her mouth moved, but no other words came out as her eyes filled with tears and her knees gave. Ellie's father grabbed her before she could fall to the floor. Swinging her up into his arms as if she weighed no more than a child, he carried her inside. Sandor ushered Ellie in after them and closed the door behind them with his foot.

His arm was still locked securely around her waist and she leaned even more heavily into him.

Helen's quiet sobs were the only sound any of them made as Ellie's dad led them unerringly into the living room. He carried Helen to the couch and gently lowered her onto it. Helen stared at him through rain drenched eyes as if she could not believe what she was seeing.

He dropped to his haunches beside the sofa and took her hand. "It is going to be okay."

But the blond woman shook her head, unending rivulets of tears rolling down her cheeks. "It can't be. I knew this day would come, but I kept hoping it wouldn't. That wasn't fair of me. I know. I've been so selfish." .

"Tell me why you took my daughter." He said it so gently that Ellie wanted to hug him.

She hadn't known he had this kind of patience and gentleness in him. Not even with his behavioral changes since his collapse.

Helen made an obvious bid for composure. "I…"

"Mom, what's going on?" ➝

Ellie felt everything inside her freeze. She spun out of Sandor's grasp to face the newcomer whose voice was so like her own. She'd already been fighting tears and now her eyes burned with them as she furiously blinked, trying to keep some semblance of control. "Amber…"

Amber was staring at her as if she was seeing a ghost. "Who are you?"

"I'm…"

"She's your sister," Helen said, her voice wobbling only a little.

"My sister?" Amber shook her head, frowning at all of them. "No. That's not possible." Her gaze shifted to her mom. "You didn't give birth to twins. I checked. I always felt like something was missing, you know? So, I checked and there wasn't another birth record. I was the only baby born to Helen and Leonard Taylor."

Ellie knew her sister was shaking inside, even though her chatter and uncracked composure gave nothing away. She was a master at hiding her emotions herself.

Sandor seemed to sense the hurricane of emotion under the surface because he took a step toward Amber, his hand out as if to help her. "Miss Taylor, perhaps you should sit down."

"Who are you?" Amber demanded, taking a step back.

"I am your sister's fiancé, Sandor Christofides."

"The shipping tycoon?"

"You read the financial pages?"

"Sometimes. When I'm bored on a shoot. And you're George Wentworth," she said to Ellie's dad, still sounding very much in command of herself.

But Ellie saw another story in the eyes that could have been her mirror. Her sister's worry for Helen Taylor was there, as well as confusion and anger that these strangers had brought obvious upset into her home.

Gently placing Helen's hand down, their father stood. "I'm…" He cleared his throat. "Yes, I'm George Wentworth."

Helen sat up, wiped at her tears and then dried her hands on her jeans and put her arms out. "Come here, baby. I have to tell you something."

Amber walked slowly toward her mother, her eyes fixed on George Wentworth as if he was a snake prepared to strike. He stepped back, moving to sit in a chair close to the sofa. It was so like how he always sat with Ellie that she felt a twinge in her heart. They were a family even if they didn't all know it yet.

Amber let her mother pull her down to sit beside her. Her gaze jumped from Ellie to her dad, back to Sandor and then finally came back to rest on Ellie. "You look just like me."

"Almost."

"Your hair is darker. You don't highlight it at all."

"No."

"It's shorter, too."

"Yes. And my eyebrows have their natural shape and I weigh at least ten pounds more than you. I don't dress as trendily and I'm not fond of running," she said, naming a pastime Hawk said that Amber spent a lot of time engaged in. "But I love old movies, we wear the same size shoe and I prefer silver over gold jewelry as well."

Helen Taylor made a sound of distress.

Amber took her hand and held it. "What's the matter, Mom?"

"Please don't hate me, Amber. I deserve it, I know I do, but I can handle anything except that."

"No one is going to hate you, Mrs. Taylor. We're going to work through this," George Wentworth said in a firm but kind tone.

Ellie was so proud of him.

"I could never hate you," Amber vowed.

Helen shook her head, her expression turning both resigned and determined. "Before you came into the room, Mr. Wentworth asked a question. He wanted…" She stopped, seemed to collect herself and went on. "He wanted to know why I'd stolen his daughter."

"What?"

The shock of the traumatic words reverberated through Amber to the room around her. Ellie could feel the shock wave hit her with physical force as her sister's whole body went stiff. Then Sandor was there, wrapping both arms around Ellie, pulling her with him to a love seat, where he tugged her down right next to him. He kept her locked tight in his protective embrace while Helen blinked back tears and took several deep breaths.

CHAPTER TWELVE

"WHEN I DID IT, I didn't think I was stealing anyone. Please believe me. I-I thought you were mine." Helen brushed the hair from Amber's temple. "I love you so much." She swallowed and then went on. "I'd lost my baby after the horrific accident that took Leonard's life and caused me to go into premature labor."

She looked at George Wentworth then, as if trying to explain what she herself found inexplicable. "Some teenagers high on pot ran a red light and plowed right into our car. I barely survived the accident. We were living near Boston at the time. They life-flighted me to the hospital from our smaller town. When my daughter died, I started haunting the baby nurseries at all the hospitals. I was there the night your wife was brought in. Everyone was running around talking about the accident. It was so much like mine. If it hadn't been so identical, I don't think it would have happened, but it was as if I was reliving it all over again.

"Everywhere around me, doctors and nurses were saying the exact same things they'd said the night of my accident. It's hard to explain, but something snapped inside me. It was as if I was living out what had happened all over again, but with a different result. I created a whole new set of memories that I could deal with better than reality. Your wife went into coma, but her babies lived. I lived, but my baby died. In my mind that night, my baby lived and she was Amber."

Ellie's dad nodded, as if he understood such a thing. Again, she felt a spurt of pride for him.

Helen turned back to Amber. "Don't ask me how I managed to get you out of the hospital because I don't remember. When I got you home, all the baby stuff was still there, I thought you were my little Amber." Her voice cracked. "I loved you so much and you were all I had left."

Amber put her arm around her mom's shoulder. "It's okay, Mom."

"It's not okay. I lived the fantasy and *believed it completely for five years*. Except for recurring nightmares of losing my baby, everything was so good. I had this overwhelming urge to move across the country, though. I thought I wanted to get away from the painful memories of your fath…I mean my husband. Later, I realized my subconscious knew that I was running from something much worse than painful memories. We moved here when you were less than a year old."

"But something made you remember," Amber said gently, her tone so like George's had been minutes before that Ellie found herself blinking back more tears.

Helen nodded. "I saw an article on George Wentworth in a business weekly." She looked around at the rest of the people in the room. "I'm a financial analyst."

"We know," George said quietly.

She swallowed convulsively and nodded. "Of course." She took another deep breath and clenched her trembling hands together. "The article mentioned the disappearance of your daughter and suddenly *I knew*. I couldn't remember taking her, but I remembered my baby dying and knew that the little girl who I loved more than my own life belonged to someone else."

"I don't understand...you would have taken me back. Mom, I know you..."

"Yes. I tried." She was looking at Amber again, her hazel eyes filled with appeal. "But when I arrived in Boston with you, I had to research George Wentworth. I couldn't give my baby over to just anyone even if he was your biological father. I was frightened of what would happen to me, but even more terrified of losing you. I was going to plead for mercy...I hoped..." She swallowed a sob. "I hoped that he would let me visit you. But when I researched him, I discovered he was a merciless shark. The article had said something about how even personal tragedy had not slowed him down businesswise. He acted as if he'd never lost a daughter and didn't notice the one he still had.

"I knew the man described in the articles I read about him and by the employees I managed to talk to would press charges and I would end up in prison. I would have faced that...but learning how he treated the daughter he still had was something else altogether. He ignored her. She was raised by nannies and servants and hardly ever saw him."

She looked at George as if she couldn't quite believe he was the man she was describing and then back to her daughter. "You were such a loving little girl and affectionate. You would have shriveled up and died under that kind of care. I couldn't do it. I couldn't give you back. And he never changed. I kept tabs and watched his daughter Eleanor be sent to boarding school when she was barely eight years old."

Helen's eyes filled with tears as she met Ellie's gaze. "It hurt so much to see you treated like that. I loved your sister with all my heart and you by proxy. I couldn't change your life, but I couldn't let your father do the same thing to Amber."

"I understand," Ellie said. And she did. Someone looking from the outside might not, but she'd lived that emotional wasteland. "I'm glad my sister escaped having a childhood like mine. I'm glad you were there to love her."

"But she needed me. If you'd given me back, we would have had each other," Amber said in a low whisper.

"I thought of that and I just couldn't sacrifice your happiness for hers." Helen buried her face in her hands and started to sob. "I'm sorry."

Ellie's dad moved to sit on the other side of Helen. He pulled her into his arms and just held her as if he alone in that room could understand her mother's pain and guilt. And perhaps it was true. If everything he'd said over the past week plus was true, he carried a load of guilt for his treatment of Ellie easily as heavy as Helen's.

"If my biological father was such a horrible man why isn't he threatening prison and yelling at her?" Amber asked Ellie, her eyes filled with a confusion Ellie understood only too well.

"He almost died a couple of weeks ago and it changed him. I think he really loves me finally and I know he's going to love you."

"But, Mom?"

"Nothing is going to happen to your mom. Dad doesn't want to hurt her and neither do I. I only want to know you. I'd like to know her, too, if she'll let me. She was a good mom to you. She took care of you and after hearing her story, I'm convinced she didn't do anything with malice."

"Are you for real?" Amber asked. "Nobody reacts like that to something like this."

Sandor laughed, hugging her. "Ellie is a special woman."

"I'm glad." The controlled facade cracked for just a second as Amber's chin wobbled. "I don't want my mom hurt."

"She won't be," George said with conviction as he continued to hold the crying woman. "She did better by my daughter than I did. I stopped looking for you after only a year. I have no excuse for that. I was a rotten father to your sister, but she loved me in spite of it."

"There are worse fathers than you were, much worse," Ellie said.

"Thank you, sweetheart, but when I remember the times your eyes so like your mother's begged me to show a spark of affection and then I didn't…I'll never forgive myself."

"You hugged me sometimes."

"I bet you remember every single time because those times were so rare."

"You really were a bastard," Amber breathed.

George flinched. "Yes. I was and I thank God, Ellie never gave up on me. I've seen the error of my ways. I want to make up for them. I think we can build a family now. All of us, if you're willing."

"I won't leave my mom out."

"Like Ellie, I would appreciate the chance to get to know her, too."

At that Helen pulled out of his arms, wiping her face. She looked ravaged, but at peace and just a little bemused. "I've been so terrified for years. I can't believe things are happening this way."

Ellie's dad grimaced. "They wouldn't have…a few weeks ago."

"It's a good thing you didn't find me then," Amber quipped.

Ellie agreed, but said nothing. The visit continued on a more positive note from there. Strangely, though, Ellie felt herself pulling into the background, listening to her dad talk with Amber and Helen. She soaked up everything they all said and enjoyed hearing it, but she couldn't participate.

If Amber felt stunned and traumatized by events, so did Ellie. She still wasn't used to having a dad that wanted to be a dad and now she had a sister and that just blew her away. She'd been alone so long, she wasn't sure how to be part of a family and she wondered in a distant part of her mind if that was one of the reasons she'd put off talking about her relationship with Sandor.

She was scared of giving in and becoming part of a family and having it all taken away again. It was the kind of fear only someone who'd lived so long on the fringes of other people's happiness could understand. Her mind worked out the disturbing thoughts as she listened to the others talk.

She learned that Amber was in town for a shoot and planned to meet back up with Miguel afterward. She was very animated when she talked about him and that made both Ellie and her dad smile. At some point, Sandor ordered dinner to be delivered. They all ate, still talking.

It was late when Sandor stood and said, "Ellie needs rest. It has been a very traumatic few weeks for her. Perhaps this visit can continue tomorrow?"

Amber looked at Ellie and bit her lip in a gesture Ellie recognized. "You haven't been talking much."

"I'm soaking it all in. I'm um…not used to being part of a family," she said, exposing one of her inner revelations.

"Our dad seems so wonderful now, it's hard to believe he raised you the way he did."

Ellie smiled. "He's not as bad as everyone is painting him."

"Yes, I was."

She shrugged. "Then it doesn't matter. You're my dad and I love you. I always have and I always will, but this family thing…it's going to take some getting used to. I like it a lot, though." She smiled again, hoping they could all read her sincerity.

Amber nodded. "I have a feeling I'm going to like you a lot, too."

"You are going to love her, just as she will love you," Sandor corrected with a warm smile. "She is infinitely lovable and it is clear you are a very special woman, too."

Ellie felt faint. Okay, that was the second oblique reference and that meant she wasn't imagining them.

Her dad cleared his throat. "I would like to stay here a while longer…to talk out what I learned from my legal counsel with Helen in regard to the kidnapping and the statute of limitations and such."

"Is everything going to be okay?" Ellie asked. "She won't go to jail?"

"She will not. I have already put efforts into motion to assure that Helen suffers no more from the tragedy of her past."

"You did that before you even met us?" Amber asked with awe in her voice.

"Yes."

"Thank you." She jumped up and hugged him.

Ellie felt a twinge…not of envy, but of sadness. She did love her dad, but she wondered if she would ever have the easy relationship with him that her sister was already developing. Even if she didn't, what they had was so much better than what she'd known growing up, she wouldn't ever moan for things to be different. She felt truly blessed. Overwhelmed, but blessed.

"Then you all don't mind if I go to the hotel?"

"No, of course not. I am very glad you have someone to take care of you like Sandor," Helen said, just as if she was Ellie's mom, too.

It was nice.

Ellie discovered that Sandor had booked them into the same room at the hotel when he followed her into it and closed the door behind them. She noticed his suitcase as well as hers had been delivered from the plane and stood against one wall side by side.

"We share a room?" she asked.

"Always."

She nodded and Sandor went very still. "What did that little nod mean?"

"What did the oblique references you've made to love today mean?" she countered.

"That I love you," he replied without hesitation.

"No. You can't."

"I assure you, I do."

"But you don't believe in love."

"Belief is not always necessary for a state of being. I learned quickly enough how much I love you when you refused to come back to me, or talk to me about our future."

"Not before then."

"I was slow, but what I lack in speed to the mark I make up for in longitude." He pulled her into his arms. "I will love you forever."

She buried her nose in his chest, breathing in the beautiful scent she associated only with him. "I thought a man loved me once, but I was wrong," she whispered against him.

"Your other lover?"

She tilted her head back to see his face. "You're so sure there has only been one?"

"Yes. Your heart is connected to sexual intimacy for you. You would not allow a man you did not love into your body and if you had loved another after him, you would have married."

"You're sure?"

"Positive. Only a fool would let you go if you loved him."

"You are so sure another man would have loved me back?"

"I am positive it is a foregone conclusion." He kissed the tip of her nose. "You are irresistibly lovable."

"He didn't think so."

"The first lover?"

"Yes."

"He was an idiot."

She nodded, having come to the same conclusion but for different reasons. "I was nineteen. He was my bodyguard. I mistook sexual pleasure for the love of a lifetime until I overheard him talking about what a score he was going to make marrying me. He wanted a piece of my dad's empire and wasn't above using me to get it. He had it all planned. He wasn't even normally a bodyguard. He was trained in business, but took the job to get close to me. Apparently everyone knew how my dad ignored me and he thought I'd be lonely and easy to seduce. He was right. He even had sex with me without protection in hopes of getting me pregnant. Thankfully it didn't happen."

Sandor's arms tightened and anger radiated off of him with palpable force. "That bastard."

"Yes, he was. He taught me a valuable lesson, though, sex is not love." Would he understand what she was asking without her actually asking anything?

"No, it is not." This time he kissed her temple and then her lips, oh so softly. "Sex is something a person can live without, but if you take your love from me, I will wither and die."

"You did not just say that," she choked.

"I did."

She shook her head.

He nodded. "Oh, yes. What happened to the bodyguard?"

"I told my dad I thought he was sexually attracted to me. That he'd made advances. He fired him. He never knew it had already gone way beyond mere attraction to final follow-through."

Sandor pulled her to bed and tumbled them both down onto it without letting her go. They remained facing each other, lying on their sides. "I am sexually attracted to you, Ellie. More than is comfortable in any sort of clothing." He illustrated by pressing an unmistakable hardness against her. "But I love you, too, *agape mou*."

"What does that mean?"

"My love."

"Oh." He'd called her that before.

"Is it my crazy man behavior before you realized you had a sister? You forgave your father far worse, can you not forgive me for accusing you of being with another man?" He really seemed agitated about it.

She cupped his cheek. "I know the pictures were damaging. If I'd argued with you, I would have convinced you it wasn't me and to help me find out who she was. I knew that. I was much angrier about your deal with my dad."

"You use the past tense. You are no longer angry?"

She shook her head with a sigh. "What would be the point? Holding onto anger just leads to bitterness and that twists a person's soul."

He didn't look appreciably comforted by that statement. "But you still do not wish to marry me?"

"I can forgive, but I don't know if I can trust and I need to trust you to marry you."

"I did not tell you about the deal because I knew it would upset you."

"You were right."

"But I would have wanted you even if your father had not made his offer. From the first moment I saw you, I wanted you. Your father noticed my interest. It was only after doing so that he made his offer."

"He told me that. He said he thought I was interested, too."

"You were."

"I was," she agreed.

"Ellie, I need you to be mine for a lifetime. You can trust me. I will never hide anything from you again."

"Because you love me?"

"Yes."

"Like with your mom?"

"Exactly."

"I'm scared, Sandor. I realized tonight that I don't know how to be part of a family. I don't know how to believe in the goodness going on around me…how to believe that you can love me." The admission hurt.

But he shook his head decisively. "You are fooling yourself to think that. Belief is something you are very good at. You had faith in your father for years when anyone else would have given up on him. You had faith in me, or you never would have come back from Spain prepared to marry me. You're a woman full of faith and I'm the man prepared to prove to you that it's grounded in something real."

"You think you can do that?"

"Give me a try."

She stared at him. It couldn't be that easy. "Is this the happily ever after from the fairy tales?"

"I am no knight, but I think, Ellie *mou*, that this is the happy beginning of two people so much in love they cannot live apart."

"You won't leave me?"

"Never."

"I won't have to be alone ever again."

"I will be your anchor and you will be my sea, surrounding me, washing over me, keeping me always with you."

"And you will stay steadily always with me."

"Yes."

"I do love you, Sandor."

"Mama said you did."

"She did?"

"Uh-huh."

"When?"

"When I cried in my coffee over losing you."

"You did not."

"I most certainly did. You can call and ask her, but later…right now I have something else in mind to do with your mouth."

She'd opened it to ask him what when he kissed her.

She'd been isolated for so long, and now she had a

family. A whole family. Warmth and gratitude filled her as her brain lost contact with reality under Sandor's loving and provoking kiss.

Ellie went back to visit her sister the next day as promised and this time, found that she could not keep quiet. They talked and talked until once again Sandor was declaring it time to return to the hotel. They stayed in Southern California for three days, returning to Boston with Helen and Amber's promise to come to visit very soon.

When Ellie and Sandor were married a month later, Amber stood up for Ellie while George Wentworth, Helen Taylor and Hera Christofides looked on in teary-eyed bliss. There was another man there. He looked familiar, but Ellie was sure she'd never met him. When he put his arm around Hera Christofides and smiled down at her, Ellie almost fainted.

She turned to Sandor right in the middle of their wedding vows and blurted, "You found your father."

"More precisely, Hawk did."

"He wasn't married."

"Never had been. Apparently when a man in our family loves, it is for a lifetime."

Joyous tears washed into Ellie's eyes as she turned back to the minister to finish repeating her vows.

But Sandor squeezed her hand before she spoke. "I also destroyed the merger contract your father and I signed."

Her knees did buckle this time and Sandor swept her up against his chest, her voluminous skirts cascading over his arms.

"You did what?" she demanded.

"Took away your last reason for doubt."

He had and she felt light-headed because of it. "But what about Dad's company?"

"I've got a lot of good years in me yet. Helen is coming to work for me as a close advisor. She's a savvy business-woman. And one day I'll have grandchildren."

Ellie looked around her from the grinning minister who didn't seem to mind the odd ceremony to the small group of people all of whom were now her family. Finally she met Sandor's possessive and adoring gaze.

She was loved and she loved in return.

She was finally part of the family she'd longed for her entire life. And it felt so very good.

She finished speaking her vows without ever looking away from the man who had in his way made all of this possible.

He was her knight in shining armor, no matter what he said and their future looked so bright she would need a new pair of sunglasses to handle it.

* * * * *

THE ROYAL HOUSE OF NIROLI
Always passionate, always proud

The richest royal family in the world—
united by blood and passion,
torn apart by deceit and desire

Nestled in the azure blue of the Mediterranean Sea, the majestic island of Niroli has prospered for centuries. The Fierezza men have worn the crown with passion and pride since ancient times. But now, as the king's health declines, and his two sons have been tragically killed, the crown is in jeopardy.

The clock is ticking—a new heir must be found before the king is forced to abdicate. By royal decree the internationally scattered members of the Fierezza family are summoned to claim their destiny. But any person who takes the throne must do so according to The Rules of the Royal House of Niroli. Soon secrets and rivalries emerge as the descendents of this ancient royal line vie for position and power. Only a true Fierezza can become ruler—a person dedicated to their country, their people…and their eternal love!

Each month starting in July 2007,
Harlequin Presents is delighted to bring you
an exciting installment from
THE ROYAL HOUSE OF NIROLI,
in which you can follow the epic search
for the true Nirolian king.
Eight heirs, eight romances, eight fantastic stories!

Here's your chance to enjoy a sneak preview of the first book delivered to you by royal decree…

FIVE minutes later she was standing immobile in front of the study's window, her original purpose of coming in forgotten, as she stared in shocked horror at the envelope she was holding. Waves of heat followed by icy chill surged through her body. She could hardly see the address now through her blurred vision, but the crest on its left-hand front corner stood out, its *royal* crest, followed by the address: *HRH Prince Marco of Niroli…*

She didn't hear Marco's key in the apartment door, she didn't even hear him calling out her name. Her shock was so great that nothing could penetrate it. It encased her in a kind of bubble, which only concentrated the torment of what she was suffering and branded it on her brain so that it could never be forgotten. It was only finally pierced by the sudden opening of the study door as Marco walked in.

"Welcome home, *Your Highness*. I suppose I ought to curtsy." She waited, praying that he would laugh and tell her that she had got it all wrong, that the envelope she was holding, addressing him as Prince Marco of Niroli, was some silly mistake. But like a tiny candle flame shivering vulnerably in the dark, her hope trembled fearfully. And then the look in Marco's eyes extinguished it as cruelly as a hand placed callously over a dying person's face to stem their last breath.

"Give that to me," he demanded, taking the envelope from her.

"It's too late, Marco," Emily told him brokenly. "I know the truth now…." She dug her teeth in her lower lip to try to force back her own pain.

"You had no right to go through my desk," Marco shot back at her furiously, full of loathing at being caught off-guard and forced into a position in which he was in the wrong, making him determined to find something he could accuse Emily of. "I trusted you…."

Emily could hardly believe what she was hearing. "No, you didn't trust me, Marco, and you didn't trust me because you knew that I couldn't trust you. And you knew that because you're a liar, and liars don't trust people because they know that they themselves cannot be trusted." She not only felt sick, she also felt as though she could hardly breathe. "You are Prince Marco of Niroli…. How could you not tell me who you are and still live with me as intimately as we have lived together?" she demanded brokenly.

"Stop being so ridiculously dramatic," Marco demanded fiercely. "You are making too much of the situation."

"Too much?" Emily almost screamed the words at him. "When were you going to tell me, Marco? Perhaps you just planned to walk away without telling me anything? After all, what do my feelings matter to you?"

"Of course they matter." Marco stopped her sharply. "And it was in part to protect them, and you, that I decided not to inform you when my grandfather first announced that he intended to step down from the throne and hand it on to me."

"To protect me?" Emily nearly choked on her fury.

"Hand on the throne? No wonder you told me when you first took me to bed that all you wanted was sex. You *knew* that was the only kind of relationship there could ever be between us! You *knew* that one day you would be Niroli's king. No doubt you are expected to marry a princess. Is she picked out for you already, your *royal* bride?"

* * * * *

Look for
THE FUTURE KING'S PREGNANT MISTRESS
by Penny Jordan in July 2007,
from Harlequin Presents,
available wherever books are sold.

HARLEQUIN Presents

THE ROYAL HOUSE OF NIROLI

Always passionate, always proud.

**The richest royal family in the world—
a family united by blood and passion,
torn apart by deceit and desire.**

Step into the glamorous, enticing world of the
Nirolian Royal Family. As the king ails he must find an
heir…each month an exciting new installment follows
the epic search for the true Nirolian king. Eight heirs,
eight romances, eight fantastic stories!

It's time for playboy prince Marco Fierezza to
claim his rightful place…on the throne of Niroli!
Emily loves Marco, but she has no idea he's a royal
prince! What will this king-in-waiting do when he
discovers his mistress is pregnant?

THE FUTURE KING'S PREGNANT MISTRESS

by Penny Jordan

(#2643)

On sale July 2007.

www.eHarlequin.com

HP12643

They're the men who have everything—except brides...

Wealth, power, charm—what else could a heart-stoppingly handsome tycoon need? In the GREEK TYCOONS miniseries you have already been introduced to some gorgeous Greek multimillionaires who are in need of wives.

Vicky knew her marriage to Theo Theakis would be purely convenient! But Theo changed the rules. He knows his wife well, and decides that her presence in his bed will be money well spent.

BOUGHT FOR THE GREEK'S BED
(#2645)

by Julia James

On sale July 2007.

REQUEST YOUR FREE BOOKS!

HARLEQUIN® *Presents*

2 FREE NOVELS PLUS 2 FREE GIFTS!

PASSION GUARANTEED SEDUCTION

YES! Please send me 2 FREE Harlequin Presents® novels and my 2 FREE gifts. After receiving them, if I don't wish to receive any more books, I can return the shipping statement marked "cancel." If I don't cancel, I will receive 6 brand-new novels every month and be billed just $3.80 per book in the U.S., or $4.47 per book in Canada, plus 25¢ shipping and handling per book and applicable taxes, if any*. That's a savings of close to 15% off the cover price! I understand that accepting the 2 free books and gifts places me under no obligation to buy anything. I can always return a shipment and cancel at any time. Even if I never buy another book from Harlequin, the two free books and gifts are mine to keep forever.

106 HDN EEXK 306 HDN EEXV

Name	(PLEASE PRINT)	
Address		Apt. #
City	State/Prov.	Zip/Postal Code

Signature (if under 18, a parent or guardian must sign)

Mail to the Harlequin Reader Service®:
IN U.S.A.: P.O. Box 1867, Buffalo, NY 14240-1867
IN CANADA: P.O. Box 609, Fort Erie, Ontario L2A 5X3

Not valid to current Harlequin Presents subscribers.

Want to try two free books from another line?
Call 1-800-873-8635 or visit www.morefreebooks.com.

* Terms and prices subject to change without notice. NY residents add applicable sales tax. Canadian residents will be charged applicable provincial taxes and GST. This offer is limited to one order per household. All orders subject to approval. Credit or debit balances in a customer's account(s) may be offset by any other outstanding balance owed by or to the customer. Please allow 4 to 6 weeks for delivery.

Your Privacy: Harlequin is committed to protecting your privacy. Our Privacy Policy is available online at www.eHarlequin.com or upon request from the Reader Service. From time to time we make our lists of customers available to reputable firms who may have a product or service of interest to you. If you would prefer we not share your name and address, please check here. ☐

HP07

HARLEQUIN®

Mediterranean N I G H T S™

Tycoon Elias Stamos is launching his newest luxury cruise ship from his home port in Greece. But someone from his past is eager to expose old secrets and to see the Stamos empire crumble.

Mediterranean Nights
launches in June 2007 with...

FROM RUSSIA, WITH LOVE
by *Ingrid Weaver*

Join the guests and crew of *Alexandra's Dream* as they are drawn into a world of glamour, romance and intrigue in this new 12-book series.

**Two billionaires, one Greek, one Spanish—
will they claim their unwilling brides?**

Meet Sandor and Miguel, men who've taken all the prizes
when it comes to looks, power, wealth and arrogance.
Now they want marriage with two beautiful women.
But this time, for the first time, both Mediterranean
billionaires have met their matches and it will take more
than money or cool to tame their unwilling mistresses!

Miguel made Amber Taylor feel beautiful for the
first time. For Miguel it was supposed to be a
two-week affair…but now he'd taken the most
precious gift of all—her innocence!

TAKEN:
THE SPANIARD'S VIRGIN

Miguel's story (#2644)

by Lucy Monroe

On sale July 2007.